The Destruction of Black

by Devin ML Andrews

1/4/25/02 GREENWOOD CHURCH TULSA, OKLAHOMA

(O.W. Gurley--Founder of Tulsa's Greenwood District)

Introduction

Greenwood, the African-American neighborhood of Tulsa, Oklahoma, was a city in and of itself. Segregated from the rest of the city, it was a neighborhood like no other. During a time when Jim Crow laws were meant to prove the supposed inferiority of Black Americans and the Black race, this community demonstrated how successful a people can be if they work together toward a common good. They bought land, built businesses, and, unlike most areas of the South, their average dollar only left the community after it circulated at least 36 times. This self-dependency became an abundant self-efficiency, and they established a since of pride in themselves as they did not trade with anyone outside the community unless absolutely necessary.

Greenwood had instilled many values into their children-- particularly, the importance of hard work, education, and the strength of the family. They believed that one could live the American dream through these three virtues. Indeed, a great many in this community were devout disciples of Booker T. Washington, who taught that civil rights and dignity were the fruits of self development. As a result, many of the teachers were paid well enough to sometimes have chandeliers in their homes. Additionally, intact nuclear and extended families were the norm--not the exception. Hence, Greenwood became the Promised Land for the African American with a dream. Not only did it boast several hundred businesses but also hospitals, movie theaters, hotels, insurance companies, and even a bus route. Even African-American millionaires made Greenwood their home. Such success thus earned this neighborhood names like Black Wall Street and Little Africa.

Even with all of these efforts, including many African-Americans enlisting to fight in World War I, they still were not extended the dignity and rights they deserved as the Grandfather Clause of 1915 prevented these hardworking Americans from voting. Hence, their rights and protection under the law were restricted, and those who built Greenwood were aware of the barriers set against them in 1919 when Greenwood residents read about Red Summer riots across the country. Still, they would not turn lose their dignity or cease their hopes to be treated equally.

Then, on June 1st, 1921, all of the efforts and successes of Black Wall Street literally went up in smoke because of the hatred, intolerance, and, moreover, envy many of the White Tulsans outside of the community. Such individuals, no doubt influenced by the Ku Klux Klan, if not members, did not see the success of Black Wall Street as a beacon of equality to be admired. Instead, the less affluent were embittered by Greenwood's wealth, and the more prosperous were jealous of their national acknowledgement. They covered their insecurities with a banner rallying White Tulsans to protect their most important and most valuable asset--their women--from the alleged savage lust of the Black man. In fact, such a banner was flown in East St. Louis, Rosewood, and all over the South. Such a banner was soaked in the blood and tears of the African-Americans fleeing or defending their communities.

    While the main characters in this novel are fictional, they represent the daily lives, dreams, fears, and hardships of the households of Greenwood. They show the pride of a people who have often been put to shame and the determination to protect what is theirs. Importantly, they present an example of the boundless things people can do when they work hard and collaborate with others even in the most tense of circumstances. This is that story.

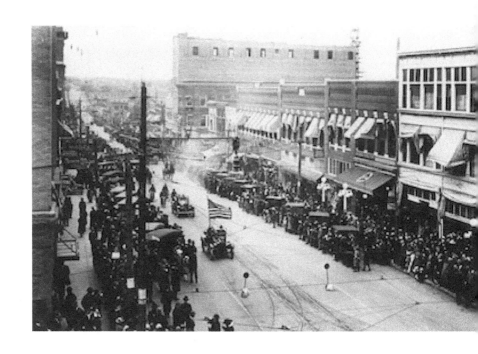

Chapter 1:
Sunday Dinner

It was a mild, sunny day on May 29, 1921. It was a Sunday, and the Mitchell family were just returning from church. They attended Vernon African Methodist Episcopal Church--the most prestigious church of the Greenwood District--the Black town within Tulsa. Clarence Mitchell, Jr., a dignified banker in his late 40s, walked arm-in-arm with his genteel wife, Violet. Both were dressed in their smart Sunday best. Mr. Mitchell wore a white three-piece suit with a club collar and formal straw hat while Mrs. Mitchell wore a spinach green dress and a large, feathery bi-corn hat. Their daughter Phyllis, a young lady, walked behind them in sky-blue dress with a navy blue sash and navy blue ribbon in her neatly pressed-and-combed hair. Both mother and daughter wore dress gloves.

"Papa?" called Phyllis, beaming.

"Yes, Phillybug?" responded Mr. Mitchell. "What is it?"

"You know that Gregory is coming for dinner tonight, right?"

"How can I forget with you pulling my ear on it every hour?" Mr. Mitchell asked sarcastically. Mrs. Mitchell chuckled with restraint.

"I can't wait for you to meet him!" she exclaimed, prancing in a circle.

"Now, Phyllis," acknowledged Mrs. Mitchell, "You know better than to act like that--particularly on a Sunday!"

"Yes, ma'am," Phyllis responded obediently, walking properly.

"I guess it is time for me to meet him--you have been meeting him for a while," responded Mr. Mitchell. "If your mama and I didn't insist on meeting him, we never would have the privilege. I only know that he is from a decent family and that he served in the war. Otherwise, I would have no knowledge of him."

"Oh, but Papa, you'll like him; I know you will. He is very brave--a corporal. He saved the life of his commanding officer and dragged injured soldiers to safety."

"He sounds mighty brave, all right," answered Mrs. Mitchell. "And handsome too, I bet. Is that so, Phyllis?" Phyllis covered her mouth and giggled.

"Mama, he is handsome, but he is also a gentleman. He holds the door for me and helps across the street."

"Those are signs of a good upbringing," said Mrs. Mitchell, looking at her husband.

"Yes, my dear," said Mr. Mitchell rolled his eyes, "Your Boston background has certainly accustomed you to know good breeding when you see it."

They strolled through Greenwood Avenue, acknowledging each of their friends and associates politely, and Phyllis' female friends catching up with them to chat and tell stories. From how the Mitchell's grasped everyone's attention, it was obvious that they were an important family and well dignified. In fact, they were well known to O.W. Gurley, J.B. Stradford, as well as their associates and friends. Indeed, Mr. Mitchell was proud of his community and all they had accomplished for themselves.

After a short while, they reached their white two-story colonial-style house. When they entered, Lela-Ann, their 60-

year-old housekeeper, a thin and short woman, came briskly from the kitchen to greet them.

"How was church, y'all?" she politely asked in her pungent Southern drawl.

"It was just fine, thank you," Mr. Mitchell responded, handing her his hat.

"Glad to hear it, sir," Lela-Ann smiled, taking his and Mrs. Mitchell's hats.

"Lela-Ann," asked Mrs. Mitchell, "I did inform you that we would be having a guest for dinner, did I not?"

"Yessum, you did."

"Excellent. Then please be sure to use the good china." Phyllis hugged her mother's arm, grinning happily. Mrs. Mitchell smiled and pat her daughter's shoulder. "Well, we have a few hours, so I need to practice my piano." She excused herself and walked into the parlor.

"Lela-Ann," asked Mr. Mitchell, "could you please bring some cool drinks into the parlor?

"Yessir," Lela-Ann turned back into the kitchen, with Phyllis trailing after.

"Lela-Ann?" asked Phyllis, as Lela-Ann retrieved a pitcher of fresh lemonade from the icebox.

"Yes, child?" asked Lela-Ann, placing the pitcher on the counter and turning to the cupboard for glasses.

"I think Gregory is going to ask Papa for permission to let me marry him tonight!"

"So, child, that's why you've been dancin' and prancin' 'round here all weekend!" Lela-Ann let out a wide-toothed grin. "Uhm-hmm! You got the fever all right!"

"Uh-huh. If he does, Papa's got to say yes! He just must!"

"Come on, child; don't get yo' self all worked up." She commenced pouring lemonade into the glasses. She was in the middle of filling the second glass, when she abruptly stopped and turned to her. "Wait a minute. You ain't in the family way, is you?"

"Lela-Ann, no! I'm pure!"

"That's good, child. That'd kill yo' mama, and it'll make yo' papa kill Gregory."

"No! It's just that, Gregory makes me feel special. I love him, Lela-Ann; I just love him!"

"That's just fine, missy. If it be the Lord's will, y'all get married soon enough!"

"I hope it is, 'cause I don't know who else I'd marry who will be as good as the Corporal Gregory Willborn!"

"Well, I'll be prayin' for ya', honey," Lela-Ann promised her. Phyllis thanked her, squeezing her tight. "Easy child! Don't make me spill this lemonade!" Phyllis released her from her grasp, and Lela-Ann picked up the tray of lemonade, taking it from the kitchen and into the parlor, where Mr. Mitchell was reading the newspaper in his chair and Mrs. Mitchell began playing *Rondo alla Turca*. Phyllis took her place at the

Baroque settee perpendicular to her father's chair while Lela-Ann handed each family member a glass of lemonade and a napkin.

When the grandfather clock in the parlor struck seven o'clock, the doorbell rang as if on cue.

"Right on time; I like that," Mr. Mitchell regally declared. As Lela-Ann approached the door, Phyllis jumped up to follow her, but Mrs. Mitchell grabbed her hand whilst still sitting.

"Phyllis, be a lady," she admonished. "A true gentleman will come to you."

"Yes, Mama," Phyllis obediently sat next to Mrs. Mitchell. She smiled at her husband while he winked at her.

"Come on in; we've been expecting you!" the Mitchell family heard Lela-Ann say. "They in the parlor." That was everyone's cue to politely stand. "Mr. Mitchell, Mrs. Mitchell, Cpl. Gregory Willborn has arrived." She stepped to the side of the parlor entryway, and in walked a tall, handsome man in an army uniform entered, bearing a bouquet of marigolds and a small box.

"Welcome, Mr. Willborn," Mrs. Mitchell greeted him.

"Thank you, ma'am," he smiled. He handed the marigolds to her. "These are for you."

"They are very beautiful!" she accepted them. "Obviously Phyllis told you that they are my favorite."

"Yes, ma'am, she sure did."

"Good evening, Gregory!" Phyllis grinned, trying to restrain her joy.

"Good evening back at you, girl!" his smile grew. Phyllis covered her mouth and giggled.

"Warm night, isn't it, son?" Mr. Mitchell joined the conversation, extending his hand for a handshake.

"It sure is, sir," he firmly shook his hand. He handed him the box. "And this is for you."

"Well, thank you," Mr. Mitchell politely smiled, accepting the box.

"Papa, aren't you going to open it?" asked Phyllis.

"All right, Phillybug, hold on," Mr. Mitchell answered. He opened the box and took a burgundy-colored tie from the wrapping.

"Oh, that is a very smart tie, Mr. Willborn," remarked Mrs. Mitchell. "Clarence, this will be a grand match for your blue suit.

"Yes, I do believe this is a nice tie," said Mr. Mitchell. "Thank you!"

"You're welcome, sir."

Suddenly, Lela-Ann reappeared.

"Dinner's ready, y'all."

"Phyllis, would you care to help Mr. Willborn to the dining room?" asked Mrs. Mitchell.

"This way," she beamed at Gregory, taking his hand and leading him out of the parlor.

"Heavenly Father," Mr. Mitchell began the grace in the dining room, "we thank you for the many blessings that you have provided us. For family, friends, and for your guiding Hand and protecting Arm, we praise you. We thank you for this food you have given us by your providence, and we ask that you consecrate it for our nourishment and enjoyment. In Jesus' Name, Amen."

"Amen," everyone responded.

Gregory looked over the abundance of food on the large table as he was sitting down: beef brisket, mashed potatoes, green beans, fried green tomatoes, and a pitcher of sweet tea. Mr. Mitchell remained standing as he reached for the cutlery and began slicing the brisket. Everyone passed their plates to him, and he placed a slice of brisket on each plate, serving himself last.

"Lela-Ann's fried green tomatoes are the greatest!" remarked Phyllis to Gregory. "We have them whenever we have company."

"They look good," answered Gregory. "I can't wait to try them!"

"I bet you don't eat like this on the base," added Mr. Mitchell.

"No, sir. It was decent, though. Filling."

"And does your family live nearby, Mr. Willborn?" asked Mrs. Mitchell.

"Yes, ma'am. They live over in Owasso. We lived there since 1912. I was actually born in Okemah, but we had to leave."

"Really? May I ask why?"

"Violet," interjected Mr. Mitchell, "You never heard what went on in Okemah years ago? That lynching?"

"Oh, yes," Mrs. Mitchell pensively placed her hand under her chin. "What a terrible thing to happen."

"Yes it was," reflected Gregory. "Papa was worried that they would turn on us too, so he packed us up and brought us to Owasso."

"What does your father do for a living?" asked Mr. Mitchell.

"He runs his own blacksmith shop, a profession that his father, a slave, taught him."

"And is this something you hope to take up someday? To become a blacksmith?"

"No, sir. It's a noble trade, blacksmith, but my father insisted on me becoming something better, so he sacrificed as much as he could to send me to Langston University to become a civil engineer."

"I like your father already!" Mr. Mitchell smiled. "My father was a slave too, but he and my mother knew that I could be more than a sharecropper in Louisiana. I can tell you, we missed many meals so that my parents could scrape to help me get through college. He sent me to Howard, but the money he saved could only pay for tuition, so two other classmates and I worked hard washing dishes at a restaurant at night to eat and to share a one room apartment. And, yes, there were hard times, but I studied Booker T. Washington who said that the Black man needed to work hard, study, and show dignity for ourselves in order to demonstrate our worth and our right to be full citizens and to be treated equally. I took this teaching to heart. I taught it to my son, who is now a student at Howard himself, studying to be a partner at my bank. I also taught it to my daughter, insisting that she lives to high standards and marries a man with high standards as well. Someone who thinks like us."

"Yes, sir."

"Well, son," interjected Mrs. Mitchell, "If you don't start eating, Lela-Ann will think you don't like her cooking!"

"Yes, ma'am," he grinned politely, picking up his fork as the family also began eating.

They all spent the hour eating and engaging in pleasant conversation about the weather and the time Booker T. Washington visited Greenwood. After Lela-Ann cleared the dinner plates to serve dessert, Gregory turned pointedly to Mr. Mitchell.

"Sir," he began, "there is something I wish to discuss with you if I may." Mrs. Mitchell tried to hide her smile. Mr. Mitchell turned to Gregory.

"You have my complete attention, Mr. Willborn," Mr. Mitchell responded.

"As your family knows my family through similar friends, you trusted me enough to let me court your daughter with our friends as escorts. We have spent much time together, and we have fallen in love. I respect your daughter very much, and I know she respects me as much as she loves me. As you are aware, I study Mr. Washington too, and have tried to live my life according to his teachings. I would also teach any of my children his teachings too. Mr. Mitchell, I with my military career and my future civil engineering career, I will be able to give your daughter everything she needs and possibly desires. Sir, I am asking for permission to marry your daughter, Phyllis."

Lela-Ann, who entered the dining room with a cake, froze in her tracks when she heard the proposal. Phyllis became so elated that she wanted to jump out of her skin, but her equally excited mother tapped on her shoulder to encourage her to settle down. Mr. Mitchell, however, was more reserved.

"You state your case very well, Corporal," he said politely, motioning for Lela-Ann to enter. She sheepishly returned to the dining room, set the cake on the table and began slicing it. "You have given me much to think about—"

"Think about what, Papa?" Phyllis interrupted.

"Young ladies never interrupt their fathers!" admonished Mrs. Mitchell.

"And, Phyllis," added Mr. Mitchell, "giving away my little Phillybug is not an easy thing to do. I must think on it—and pray. I will need a day. What are your plans for tomorrow morning?"

"I am free for the holiday, sir."

"Good. Come by at noon, and I will have an answer for you."

"Yes, sir, I will certainly do that!"

"This way, Phyllis will be home from the boutique," said Mrs. Mitchell.

"Yes, " reflected Mr. Mitchell. "I forgot that Widow Sampson would be opening her shop half day tomorrow." He turned to Gregory. "I'm sure Phyllis told you that she is being trained as a couturier."

"Yes," Gregory answered, "She did tell me she has been learning to make dresses and hats."

"Should my husband accept your proposal, Mr. Willborn," asked Mrs. Mitchell, " Will you allow her to continue this trade?"

"If it makes her happy, and if she can still contribute to the household, it would be wrong of me to try to stop her."

"That is good to hear, Mr. Willborn," Mrs. Mitchell smiled reservedly. "Still, Phyllis has been taught what her duties are as a young lady. While being a couturier has always pleased her, since she was little, she knows the importance of sacrifice. She knows that her career must never allow her to neglect her most importance duties as a wife: raising children and keeping a happy home. That is what my mother taught me, and that is what I hope Phyllis will teach her daughters."

"Yes, ma'am," responded Gregory. "If I am not being too forward, may I ask where you hail from? I don't know anyone around here who speaks as properly as you do."

"Thank you for the complement! Actually, I am from Boston. My family lived in Boston as Free Blacks for two generations before me."

Lela-Ann handed everyone a slice of cake, walked to the kitchen, and returned with a pot of coffee.

"So, you are from Boston, and Mr. Mitchell is from Louisiana? Those are two completely different worlds. It must have been fate that the two of you should meet."

"I call it God's Providence. I actually met him in Washington, D.C. A cousin was graduating from Howard, and Mr. Mitchell was in his same class. I ran into him at the ceremony and again in Atlanta when I went to Spelman the year after. He was trying to get a job as a banker, but there were not many Black banks in Atlanta at the time, and most White banks would only hire him to mop the floor. He was able to etch out a living for himself by working as an accountant for the Black upper class of the city. He even met THE Alonzo Herndon! He also taught Economics at local high schools."

"They were hard times," interjected Mr. Mitchell, "But they taught me an important lesson. The Negro must not wait for the White population to give him anything of value. If he truly wants it, he must get it for himself through hard work and sacrifice. I worked hard those years, but I also saved and sent home money when I could. The best thing about Atlanta was getting to know Mrs. Mitchell here. Still, we both wanted something more. Then we read about how Negroes were building their own towns and communities here in Oklahoma, and we knew that this state is where people like us could flourish. So, after Mrs. Mitchell graduated from Spelman, we married and moved here."

"That is truly remarkable, sir. That sounds just like how my mama and papa decided to come here. In fact, my grandfather brought us to Oklahoma in the Land Rush."

Lela-Ann handed him a cup and saucer of coffee that she poured, and Gregory accepted with gratitude. He looked at his slice of cake. "Caramel! My favorite!"

"Phyllis made certain Lela-Ann and I understood that!" smiled Mrs. Mitchell.

After everyone devoured their coffee and cake, Gregory took his leave, both Lela-Ann and Phyllis helping him to the door. As if on cue, Phyllis excused herself for the evening, going up to her room to prepare for bed. While Lela-Ann cleared the dishes in the dining room, Mr. and Mrs. Mitchell returned to the parlor, where they discussed their college memories and their life together in Oklahoma. Naturally, they also discussed their impressions of Cpl. Gregory Willborn and whether he would be a proper match for Phyllis.

Chapter 2:
Memorial Day Joy

The next day, Gregory arrived at the Mitchell home precisely at noon. Upon rising the doorbell, Lela-Ann strolled to answer the door, but Phyllis walked very quickly and ladylike, beating her to the door. She then reached for the doorknob, but Lela-Ann gently slapped her hand.

"Now, you know what your Mama would say!" she scolded.

"Yes, ma'am," she stepped away from the door as Lela-Ann opened it and allowed Cpl Willborn, who stepped inside.

"Good afternoon, Corporal!"

"Good afternoon, Miss Lela-Ann," he politely nodded to her. He then turned to Phyllis. "Hello there, girl!"

"Hello, Gregory," Phyllis beamed up at him. They both held out their arms for an embrace, but at the clearing of Lela-Ann's throat, they both looked at her disapproving gaze and let their arms drop. She smiled and nodded her head at them.

"Mr. Mitchell be expectin' you," she told Gregory. "He in the study. I'll go get him." She then walked over to the study door and knocked on it. Being instructed to enter, she opened the door and walked halfway in, announcing Gregory's arrival. Being given her instructions, she exited the study and left the door slightly open. "You can go in."

"Thank you, Miss Lela-Ann," he replied. Straightening his suit, he walked confidently into the study and shut the door. Mr. Mitchell, who was reading his newspaper, folded the paper and placed it on his desk.

"How are you today, son?" he asked.

"I'm doing fine, sir."

"Please, have a seat." Gregory sat at the chair in front of the desk. "I have been giving your proposal much thought. You seem like a decent young man and I have only heard good things about you." He retrieved a cigar box from his desk drawer. He removed a cigar from the box, then lit it with his lighter and began to smoke. "I have always hoped that my daughter would marry someone who is not only well-off, but also a man who is educated and respectful. Someone who believes in the teachings of Booker T. Washington. Do you smoke?"

"From time to time, sir."

"Well then," he opened the cigar box and held it to Gregory, "take one."

"Thank you, sir," Gregory accepted a cigar, and Mr. Mitchell lit it for him.

"Of course. If you only smoke on occasion, then this is the best occasion to do it, is it not? After all, becoming engaged to my daughter is a grand occasion, indeed!" Gregory's eyes became as large as saucers.

"Sir," a grin growing on his face," are you saying--"

"A brave war hero," interrupted Mr. Mitchell, "a bright and educated young man with a promising future would be a welcome addition to our family! Yes, of course you have my permission." Both men rose from their seats.

"Thank you very much, sir! I promise you that you will not regret it." They both shook hands vigorously.

"I know I won't. Welcome to the family, Gregory!" They both stood and took a few puffs. "Well, son, shall we go tell the womenfolk?"

"Good idea." Mr. Mitchell pat Gregory on the back as they both walked to the door. As soon as he opened it, both he and Gregory were befuddled to see Mrs. Mitchell, Phyllis, and Lela-Ann standing by the door. "What the devil are you gals doing here? Were you eavesdropping?"

"Now, Clarence," answered Mrs. Mitchell, "How could I listen? That door is so thick, you couldn't even hear a baby cry from out here.

"The way that boy grinnin' over there," added Lela-Ann, "Either you said yeah, or he needs the water closet."

"All right, all right," said Mr. Mitchell. "I did in fact give my permission for the two of you to marry." Phyllis squealed with delight and wrapped her arms around Mr. Mitchell.

"Thank you, Papa! You've made me so happy."

"I want you to be happy. Still, you can be married for 20 years and have 10 children, but you will always be my Phillybug."

"Of course, I will, Papa."

"Lela-Ann," said Mrs. Mitchell, "why don't you go and get that bottle of brandy we have been saving?"

"Right away, ma'am." Lela-Ann turned and left.

"So, Mr. Willborn, I mean, Gregory," began Mrs. Mitchell, "Will the two of you be living on base when you marry?"

"I'm not sure, ma'am," answered Gregory. "Except for barracks, there is very limited housing for Negroes."

"Damn shame, isn't it, son?" reflected Mr. Mitchell. "You save lives and show bravery, yet they don't think you are even good enough for decent housing."

"Clarence, there's no need for language," admonished Mrs. Mitchell.

"Excuse me, my dear."

"It is a great shame," weighed in Gregory, "But I'm not going to make a fuss over it. I will just find a place outside of the base,"

"We won't hear of it," said Mr. Mitchell. "Once the two of you are married, you will stay here until you can get a house. I insist."

"Thank you, sir."

"Thank you so much, Papa!" Phyllis wrapped her arms around her father.

"Of course!" Mr. Mitchell returned the embrace. "I'm not giving you up that quickly!"

"We must set a date," began Mrs. Mitchell. "Gregory, do you attend Vernon?"

"No, ma'am," answered Gregory. "My family attends St. John."

"That church on Lansing, near Pine?" asked Mr. Mitchell.

"That's the one."

"I've heard many good things about that congregation," Mr. Mitchell replied. "Still, it would make her mother and me very happy if you would have the wedding at our church. Very important people go there. Besides, it's tradition for the one who pays the piper to call the tune, if you understand my meaning."

"I believe I do, sir," answered Gregory. "I think this would be acceptable."

"Very good, then," Mr. Mitchell pat him on the back. Lela-Ann then returned with a silver tray, holding a crystal brandy decanter and four crystal glasses. She placed the tray on the dining room table. "Thank you, Lela-Ann, but I think you forgot a glass."

Lela-Ann looked up at Mr. Mitchell, confounded.

"How that be, Mr. Mitchell?" she asked. "There's only four o' y'all. 'Less'n you be 'spectin' company?"

"Lela-Ann," Mr. Mitchell spoke to her in a reprimanding tone, a crooked smile growing, "you forgot YOUR glass." Everyone turned to her, beaming.

"Mine, sir?"

"Why, certainly! Now you go and get another one of those crystal glasses. Go on, now!" Mr. Mitchell waved her towards the kitchen.

"I'll be right back, y'all!" Lela-Ann hurried towards the kitchen.

"Why, Clarence," Mrs. Mitchell clasped onto her husband's arm, "I do believe you have made her day." Mr. Mitchell patted his wife's hand.

"Lela-Ann has been taking care of us since Phyllis was a sprout," Mr. Mitchell answered his wife. "She treats us like family, and it's high time we treated her the same. Moreover, I think she should take meals with us at the table from now on."

"I think that's a fine idea, Papa," extolled Phyllis.

Lela-Ann, carefully holding a crystal glass identical to the others, rejoined the family.

"I don't think I ever had me no liquor in more than 30 years. Lordy, I hope it don't swoon me."

"You'll do just fine," Phyllis smiled at her.

Lela-Ann put her glass next to the others and took the top off of the decanter. She poured a glass of brandy for each person, starting with Mr. Mitchell, pouring a glass for herself last. Mr. Mitchell then raised his glass, with the others following suit.

"To Phyllis and Gregory!" he toasted. "May God give you happiness, prosperity, and--please, Lord--a son!" Everyone toasted and sipped their drinks.

"Oh, Gregory," said Phyllis dreamily, holding onto her fiancé, "this is the happiest day of my life."

"Well, don't get settled yet, girl," answered Gregory, "Because we've got many more to come." Mrs. Mitchell smiled and took Mr. Mitchell's hand, who in turn wrapped his arm around her.

"Why are the two of you standing around here?" asked Mr. Mitchell. "Why don't you too go for a stroll? It's a beautiful day."

"That's a good idea," Gregory said. "Let's go get some air." Both Gregory and Phyllis left the house.

"It does my heart good to see our daughter so happy!" Mrs. Mitchell remarked, walking towards the parlor.

"Yes, indeed," replied Mr. Mitchell, joining her. "Too bad Junior is away at college. He'd love to see his sister get engaged. I'll write to him tonight. And Gregory? I have high hopes for him." He sat in his chair as Mrs. Mitchell sat at her piano.

"Of course you do," said Mrs. Mitchell, playing a piece from Chopin. "I just knew you'd say yes to him." She glared her husband with her knowing smile.

"Is that so?" Mr. Mitchell feigned indignation. "And if I said no?"

"I'd have telephoned your friend, the good Dr. A.C. Jackson, and have him come over to check your vitals!" They both laughed. "But still, we should think of a good date for the wedding."

"Well, Violet," responded Mr. Mitchell, "when you and I were to be married, my old pappy, Nate Mitchell, told me to take the number of months we knew each other and multiply it by three, and then add that to the day of the proposal. That's if she wasn't in the family way. If she was, just do it before she shows!" They both laughed.

"Oh, stop your vile talk, Clarence!" she said between chuckles.

"Seriously, though," Mr. Mitchell continued, "That would put the wedding in February."

"Who likes going to weddings in the winter?" demanded Mrs. Mitchell.

"Well, I doubt the summer is enough time, but making them wait until next spring might tempt them to sin."

"In other words, your father is of little help to us now."

"I think I know what to do. We can set the wedding for six months from now. That would mean...late October. The weather will still be decent, I reckon."

"I think that's a great idea, Clarence!" beamed Mrs. Mitchell.

"Lela-Ann!" Mr. Mitchell called.

"Yessir?" Lela-Ann promptly entered the parlor.

"Go in my study and bring me my calendar, please!"

"Yessir! Planning the wedding, huh?"

"We certainly are," Mrs. Mitchell replied.

"I'll go get the calendar." Lela-Ann departed.

Suddenly, the front door opened, and in walked Gregory and Phyllis entered. Both had worried expressions as they walked into the parlor. Mrs. Mitchell, upon looking at their faces, stopped playing the piano.

"What's with the two of you?" asked Mrs. Mitchell. "You were walking on clouds when you left here a moment ago. "

"Mr. Mitchell," spoke Gregory, "do you know a man called Dick Rowland?"

"That bootblack who works downtown? I know him all right. Why do you ask?"

"He may be in a little trouble, sir. White folk downtown are growing mad as hell, saying he had gotten fresh with a White girl who runs the elevator at the Drexel Building. A colored man from the neighborhood says he saw a man who looks just like Dick running from the building as he heard a girl screaming."

"I approved a loan for his uncle to open a barbershop last week. Dick Rowland's a good boy. I'm sure there's a reasonable explanation."

"Sir, I heard White folks talking. They aren't interested in explanations. They want a lynching."

"Son, don't overreact. Rowland is fairly well known. Even by the Whites. I'm sure this can be cleared up."

"I really hope so, Papa," said Phyllis. "We heard some White men talking about teaching 'niggers' a lesson to keep them from touching White women. They looked at me and started saying such disgusting things that I cannot repeat. Gregory started walking over to them, but I begged him to ignore them because I didn't want him to get killed."

"Damn crackers think they can treat our women anyway they want," Gregory bitterly stated.

"Now Gregory," admonished Mrs. Mitchell, "we don't use that language in this house."

"Sorry, ma'am."

"You were right," said Mr. Mitchell, standing up and walking to Gregory, "in defending your fiancée. Still, you've got to learn to turn the other cheek with these people. Not just because it says so in the Bible, but also because if you don't, they won't think twice about taking your head. We've made good strides here in Greenwood, and many of them hate us for it. They hate us because they thought we would become destitute without them and that we are only fit to be slaves. Our hard work and successes took their prejudice and their feelings of superiority and threw them right back in their faces."

"Even with our hard work, they still think they are better than us and that we are just uppity. And you, sir, I know some of those White folks still refer to you as 'that nigger banker.' I still see White privates sneering at me—a superior officer. Superior at what? And, Mr. Mitchell, imagine what they could have done to Phyllis if I weren't there!"

"But you were there—to protect her!" insisted Mr. Mitchell.

"Everyone, let's not discuss this any further," Mrs. Mitchell weighed in. "We are all safe, and that is what matters. As for Dick Rowland, there are enough decent people in this town, Colored or White, who understand that he is a good boy who has better sense than to get fresh with any girl, let alone a White one. I'm sure nothing will come of this incident."

"Yes, Mrs. Mitchell," sullenly replied Gregory.

"I hope you're right, Mama," said Phyllis.

"Your mother is certainly right," Mr. Mitchell assured her.

"Since both of you are back from your walk," Mrs. Mitchell changed the subject, we should plan the wedding. Your father and I thought October would be a grand month..."

Chapter 3:
The Tide Changes

The next morning, Tuesday, May 31, 1921, was the same as any other. The paperboy delivered the issue of Tulsa Star, the Colored newspaper. Mr. Mitchell, who arose briefly before dusk, retrieved said newspaper, fully dressed, and then walked to the dining table, where Lela-Ann poured him his first cup of coffee. He thanked her, took a sip, and began reading his paper as Lela-Ann walked to the kitchen to prepare breakfast, leaving Mr. Mitchell the pot of coffee.

Mrs. Mitchell and Phyllis were still asleep in their beds, only the smell of coffee perking Mrs. Mitchell to arise. She left her bedroom, walked over to Phyllis' door, and rapped vigorously on it, bidding her daughter to wake up. After Phyllis answered her mother, Mrs. Mitchell returned to her room and picked something to wear. Back in the dining room, Mr. Mitchell sipped leisurely on his coffee whilst reading the paper. He would have, just like every morning, his second cup when his family joined him. Indeed, this was a typical start to a typical day for the Mitchell family. Unbeknownst to them, this was the last morning they would spend in their comfortable home.

"So, Gregory was given permission to live off-base," declared Phyllis. "He still will move in after we are married, but he wants to live closer to here."

"That's a good idea," remarked Mr. Mitchell, folding his paper.

"I think he will move into Ms. Jones' boarding house. I can't wait to see how his room looks!"

"You won't be going there alone, Ms. Mitchell," declared Mrs. Mitchell. "Not without one of us as a chaperone."

"But, Mama, we won't be doing anything wrong. And we are to be married."

"It's no matter, dear. Young ladies never go to a man's apartment by herself."

"Oh, bother, Mama—"

"Don't quarrel with your mother, Phillybug," admonished Mr. Mitchell. "She's right. A girl all alone in a boy's apartment is too much temptation for both of them. No daughter of mine is going to have relations outside of marriage. Until you both say 'I do,' none of you will.' Is that clear?"

"Yes, sir."

"That's my girl," Mr. Mitchell patted her hand. He then reached in his pocket and checked his pocketwatch. "I'd better get going. Violet, I will walk to work today, so you can use the Brisco if you need it."
"Thank you," Mrs. Mitchell responded as Mr. Mitchell left his seat to kiss his wife and child goodbye.

"I have an idea," Mrs. Mitchell turned to Phyllis after Mr. Mitchell left, "Once Gregory finds a room and moves in, let's go shopping. We can get him some curtains or some sheets. Or we can telephone his mother and plan something. That way, you can see your fiancé's quarters under chaperone. Fair?"

"Excellent idea, Mama! If I may, I'd like to make the curtains. Widow Sampson taught me how last month."

"Then you should make them!" smiled Mrs. Mitchell. "That would be a nice treat for Gregory."

"Oh, Mama, I love you and Papa so much! I'm actually getting married!"

"We love you too, dear. And I am sure we will eventually love Gregory too. He is a fine man. You've done well! Now, finish your breakfast and get ready for work! Breakfast is the wife's most important meal. It gives her the energy to do all of her tasks for the day, and it helps her to take good care of her children."

"Yes, Mama."

Mr. Mitchell, wearing a three-piece suit and a derby hat, walked cheerfully to his bank, greeting all of his neighbors along the way. He had come to know all many of the residents of Greenwood, and they respected him. They were fellow congregants at Vernon AME. They were shopkeepers and restaurateurs he granted loans to with very little collateral but with a goal for success. There were always children coming to his house, sent by their parents to receive piano lessons from Mrs. Mitchell. As far as he was concerned, no one played the piano like his Violet, and he was confident that the only thing that kept her from teaching at Juilliard was the color of her skin.

As he walked to the door of his bank, Mitchell & Company Savings and Loan, he approached one of his partners, Maxwell Lewis, as he was unlocking the door.

"Good morning, Lewis!" he grinned. "I see you also had the notion to come in early."

"Is it a good morning, Mitchell?" Mr. Lewis looked at him with weariness in his eyes.

"What kind of question is that? What's wrong?"

"You didn't hear? They arrested that Rowland boy! Picked him up early this morning."

"What?" Mr. Mitchell's face dropped. "On what charge?"

"They say he tried to rape that White girl."

"That's outrageous! That boy is too smart to even look a White woman in the eye, let alone attack her. Where did you hear this?"

"My wife Eula received a call from her aunt who saw the police taking him away in irons. It's the truth. They better get him out of Tulsa before White folks start getting crazy. You remember what happened to that White boy who killed that cab driver last year? A mob dragged him from the county jail and lynched him. If they have the gumption to lynch a White man, what do you think they will do to a Colored man?"

"I doubt I want to know. But Lewis, things look peaceful right now. Let's just hope things stay that way."

"You mean, let's pray."

"Let's pray. And, while we pray, let's work!" The men both walked into the bank.

Meanwhile, Gregory was on base, eating breakfast in the Colored mess hall. He was at a table with other Colored officers, and they too were discussing the arrest of Dick Rowland.

"I hope they keep that boy safe," said a sergeant in his 30's, sitting next to Gregory. These White folks will try to kill us just for being in the wrong place in the wrong time." He pointed to a scar on his face. "You see this? I got this in Chicago two years ago getting off a trolley. A group of crazy, bloodthirsty crackers started chasing me, throwing bricks and rocks at me. The corner of a brick got me in the face and almost got my eye. Good thing I could run, or I wouldn't be sitting here talking about it."

"Run, nigga, run," lamented another officer.

"But you can't run in a jail cell," added the sergeant.

"You can still fight," said Gregory. "Even if you are still bound to die, you can try to take one with you. A man who served with me, Homer Johnson, wrote to me how two White men tried to corner him during that riot in Charleston. He only had a knife, but he gutted both of those animals like fish."

"Then he's one lucky brother," concluded a fourth officer. "Lucky he didn't get killed and lucky he didn't go to jail."

"But why do we always need to run and hide?" protested Gregory, "Why do we need to be ashamed? We stuck our necks out for this damned country, and we can't even share mess halls with the White soldiers. And you?" he turned to the sergeant, "how many Colored sergeants are there in this country? And still, you can't even walk down a street up North, even in uniform, without being attacked. Back in the Great War, I sometimes didn't know who was the real enemy: the German or the White American soldier."

"I hear you man," responded the second officer, "but why would you want to eat with the White soldiers? Here, you can eat with those who respect you and your rank, and you are left in peace. If you try to eat with them White boys, they will either move away from you or pull pranks on you. Even the privates won't hesitate to call you a nigger. If they would give us the supplies we need as quick as they do for the White soldiers, I would be happy."

"So, 'separate, but equal', huh?"

"Damn right! You need to read some Marcus Garvey, man. What he says is the truth. We are not going to get the respect and rights we deserve in the country. No matter how much we fight in their wars or act like good niggers, it just won't work. Our place is Africa, and we need to carry our black hides across that ocean while we still can."

"I don't know about y'all," said Gregory, "but I'm not going anywhere. This country is more ours than it is theirs. We were brought over by force to work the land they took from the Indians. Our blood is in the cement that built the White House. It's in the cotton fields, and on the battlefields too."

"Yet, that cotton's still white, ain't it?" joked the fourth officer. All the men laughed.

"Shut up!" said Gregory, also laughing. Suddenly, the lieutenant, a White man, entered the quarters. The sergeant, who noticed the lieutenant, rose to his feet.

"Attention!" shouted the sergeant. The officers and privates quickly rose and stood erect, their arms to their sides.

"As you were," said the lieutenant. "Men, some of you may have heard, but a local Colored boy was picked up this morning for trying to rape a female White civilian. There may or may not be trouble over this, but if you must leave base, either for duty or after knock off, be on guard, and don't instigate anything. Is that clear?"

"Yes, sir!" responded the men.

"Good. Get ready to begin duty in 20 minutes. Good day men."

"Good day, sir!" The lieutenant exited the mess hall.

"Now, boys, if a Northern lieutenant is worried about trouble, " said Gregory, "it stands to reason some of the good old boys are up to something, don't it?"

"You ain't lyin'," answered the fourth officer.

"So, what are we gone do?" asked the first officer.

"Nothing!" the sergeant spoke up. "You heard the lieutenant. Y'all remember what happened at Camp Logan during the war, don't you?"

"That whole trial was a sham," said Gregory.

"It doesn't matter. They hung 13 soldiers for defending themselves against those crackers who gave them hell. I don't want any men in this unit to go out looking for trouble."

"Yes, sir," the officers answered.

"All right, then. Finish your breakfast and get to work."

A few hours passed, and the while Mr. Mitchell and Gregory were about their business, their concern for the safety of Dick Rowland never departed their minds. Gregory did his best to distract himself with training a squad assigned to him and assisting the sergeant, and so did Mr. Mitchell. At lunch time, he called his associates, including Dr. A.C. Jackson and even O.W. Gurley, to discuss the matter. They intended to keep in touch for the rest of the day and then meet to advocate for Mr. Rowland. He even called a few White attorneys he considered allies to get their perspective. All they could do was assure him that Rowland would be released because they knew he was "a good boy." Mr. Mitchell tried to soothe himself with the superficial confidence that a few good words from the more prominent White Tulsans would keep Rowland safe.

   Meanwhile, Phyllis was busy working with Widow Sampson in her boutique. She was busy with preparing a dress for the local bishop's daughter's debutante ball while Widow Sampson was having coffee with a friend who had just placed an order for a church hat. Suddenly, Willy, Widow Sampson's 18 year old nephew, quickly burst into the shop in a panic. He was holding a newspaper.

"Young man," Widow Sampson, a woman in her sixties scolded, "You know better than to run in here like you've got no sense!"

"I'm sorry ma'am," he panted.

"What's the matter, son?" Widow Sampson's face softened with concern.

"They gon' string that boy up!"

"What boy? Dick Rowland?" Willy, still panting, gave her the paper. She looked at the cover story of the afternoon issue of Tulsa Tribune, and her mouth dropped in shock. Speechless, she handed the paper to her friend. Curious, Phyllis came over and looked over the woman's shoulder. She began to feel nauseous when she read the headline in question.

NAB NEGRO FOR ATTACKING GIRL IN AN ELEVATOR

"Oh, no!" said Phyllis, starting to tremble. This can't be happening. Not now!"

"Honey, it can happen anytime, and anywhere," Widow Sampson said, bitterly. "They don't even care if he's guilty. I see how those rednecks look at us. We have always worked hard, but this time, we are working hard to make ourselves wealthy and not the Anglo-Saxons. They hate us because we have what they want. Even the poorest ones living in soddies outside of town think they are better than Mr. Gurley, and they are looking for any excuse to bring us down."

"You listen to her, girl," said Widow Sampson's friend, a woman 10 years her senior.

"Yes, Ms. Jamison."

"And I know all about how that cracker, Richard Lloyd Jones, hates us Negroes! He is probably Grand Wizard of Tulsa, the degenerate!" She held out her hand to her friend for the paper, and she unreservedly gave it to her. "So I will show you where all Klan manifestos belong!" She walked over to her cast-iron wood stove, opened the glass door, and tossed the paper inside. Everyone watched as the paper engulfed in flames.

"And good riddance!" added Ms. Jamison.

"Don't you worry," said Phyllis. "Papa believes he is innocent, and he knows all the important men in Greenwood and even some of the important White men in Tulsa. He won't let Mr. Rowland get hurt."

"I sure hope you're right," answered Ms. Jamison, shaking her head. "These old eyes have seen some terrible things, so I just don't know. I just don't know."

"I've got a bad feeling," said Widow Sampson. "I think I need to close up early. Willy, you see Phyllis home."

"I don't live too far," insisted Phyllis. "I'll be all right."

"Don't argue with me girl," Widow Sampson said, sullenly. "Pretty Colored girl like you is not safe out there alone on a day like this.

"Yes, ma'am."

"Come on, I'll see you home," said Willy. Phyllis left the boutique with him.

The boutique was just at the edge of Greenwood, so when Phyllis and Willy stepped outside, they could see the Whites of Tulsa across from them, as if the street that divided them was the gulf separating one world from the next. Phyllis looked from the corner of her eye at the White residents, earnestly reading their copies of the Tulsa Tribune.

"I knew this would happen," said one woman, whose husband just read the story to her as they walked. "That nigra thought he was good enough to mount a White woman and wouldn't take no for an answer."

"I tell you, them niggers are becoming too big for their britches," her husband answered.

"Their money is not enough for them, so they have to take our women too," said another White man to his business associate. "We've got to do something."

"That's where that monkey lives," said a father to his young son. "That place may look good, but any man in there would force himself on your sister, making her give birth to pickaninnies." The little boy stuck his tongue out at Willy.

"Willy," said a nervous Phyllis, tugging Willy's arm, "Let's get out of here. Let's go." A few White teen boys, with trouble on their faces, started to approach them. Willy noticed them too.

"Yeah, let's go," Willy responded, grabbing Phyllis' arm.

"Well, look what we have here!" said the taller one with a lustful smile. "A fine drink of nigger water!"

"I'll have me some of that!" said the other White boy. He turned to Willy. "Go home, boy."

"This is the daughter of Mr. Mitchell, the banker," Willy bravely answered "I'm taking her home."

"Oh, we'll take her home, don't worry!" said the taller boy.

"Yeah," said the shorter boy, starting to unbutton his shirt.

"O God, no!" cried a frightened, virginal Phyllis, hiding behind Willy.

"I can't let you do that, sir," responded Willy. "I'm supposed to get her home safely."

"Don't give me no sass, boy!" the taller boy raised his voice. "Besides, if she'll be good, we won't hurt her. Now, get on out of here, boy!" He pulled Willy away from Phyllis and grabbed Phyllis's hand before she could escape."

"No!" she screamed. "Take your hands off me!"

"Don't talk back to me, gal!" he yelled, pulling her closer to him. "We're gonna teach you niggers about being so uppity. When we get done with you, the next buck's gonna think twice about raping a White woman!"

"Leave her alone!" yelled Willy, punching him in the jaw. The shorter White boy kicked Willy in the back, knocking him down. He then put his foot on the back of Willy's neck.

"Stay down, boy, or I'll snap your neck!" the shorter White boy warned. Willy relented.

"All right, that's enough!" said a Colored man in his forties, holding a pistol. Another Colored man came too, pointing a shotgun at the boys. He was joined by two other men who were holding pistols. One of the men who pointed his pistol at the shorter boy spat out his tobacco. The shorter boy removed his foot from Willy's neck, and the taller boy released Phyllis. Willy, furious and emboldened, quickly stood up and shoved the shorter boy to the ground. Phyllis ran over to Willy and buried her face in his chest, sobbing.

"Come on, it's all right!" said the taller boy, his hands in the air. "We were just having fun." The shorter stood up and walked backwards to his friend, his hands also in the air.

"Fun, huh?" remarked the man with the shotgun. "Didn't look like that to me. What it looks like is you getting your head blown off if you don't head on down that road and stay away from us. Now, git!"

"Come on, let's get out of here!" said the shorter boy as they began to run.

"We'll take care of them later!" said the taller boy as they ran away.

"Y'all all right?" asked the first man with the pistol.

"Thank you so much!" Phyllis hugged the man with the shotgun.

"Ain't nothing, sugar," the man answered. "Men take care of their women."

"Y'all need to get home now," said the second man with the pistol. "There might be trouble tonight."

"Sirs, thank you," said Willy, walking away with Phyllis. The men with the guns tarried a little to joke about the two boys they drove off.

Mrs. Mitchell was just concluding a piano lesson with a 10 year old girl while Lela-Ann was dusting around the parlor.

"Good work, today!" Mrs. Mitchell praised her student. "You will be more than ready for tour recital next week. Your mother and father will be so proud!"

"Thank you, Mrs. Mitchell! Do you think I could be a virtuoso when I grow up?"

"There's no doubt in my mind, young lady. All the same, you should aim for more. You should go to college and become a teacher or even a doctor. Who knows? Maybe you can start a music school like Julliard!"

"That would be wonderful!" beamed the girl.

"It sure would. Now, go call your mother so that she can pick you up."

"Yes, ma'am." She stood up from the piano bench and walked to the telephone in the hallway.

"I think she could be a professional one of these days, Mrs. Mitchell!" said Lela-Ann. Mrs. Mitchell nodded proudly.

"She certainly could. But, it's also important to have something to fall back on." She answered. Suddenly, the door opened. Lela-Ann put down her duster and walked to the hallway. In walked Willy and a stricken Phyllis.

"Lord God, child!" Lela-Ann exclaimed. "What happened to you?" Mrs. Mitchell, alerted, entered the hallway.

"Phyllis?" she said. "What's the trouble? What happened?"

"Ma'am," explained Willy, "Two White boys stopped us and—"

"Did they ravish her?" Lela-Ann asked, horror on her face.

"No, ma'am. They wanted to though. They said they wanted to teach us a lesson for raping one of their women. I fought them best I could, but they wouldn't leave us alone until a group of men came with guns and scared them off."

"And who are you?" Lela-Ann asked. Mrs. Mitchell looked closer at him. Her eyes softened.

"Why, you're Widow Sampson's nephew. Thank God you were there. Lord knows what might have happened if you weren't." At this, Phyllis covered her face and sobbed loudly.

"What did I do? I just wanted to get home! I'm no one's whore; I'm the banker's daughter! That doesn't matter to them! They think they can do anything they want to me, and in broad daylight! It's just wrong, it's just wrong, it's just wrong!"

"Oh, my darling baby!" Mrs. Mitchell hugged her inconsolable daughter tightly. "It's going to be all right!"

"No it won't! We are just animals to them! Animals they can do anything to!"

"Sweetheart, hush now. You are safe. You are with your family. Come upstairs; you need rest." She turned to Lela-Ann. "Could you bring up some warm milk? And get Willy something to eat in the kitchen."

"Yes, ma'am," said Lela-Ann.

"And again, Willy, thank you!"

"Thank you, ma'am." Willy answered as Mrs. Mitchell led her daughter up to her bedroom.

"Yeah, they was gon' rape her," said Lela-Ann to Willy in the kitchen. "No doubt about that. Now, I never told nobody this, but when I was a young girl down in Alabama, these two crackers got me when I was on the road going to school. And

I was 12 years old. They wasn't avengin' no rape of a White woman then. Naw, honey, they picked me because they saw me holding books. 'Watcha doin' wit them books, gal?' they said. 'You don't need to read and write to pick cotton.' I tried to ignore them like Daddy taught me, but that made them mad. They got out of their buggy to teach me a lesson. They did me so bad, I could never have no chilluns. Child, I didn't try to find no man my whole life. Just didn't see the point. But yeah, when a White man look at a Colored girl that way, unbuttoning his shirt too, every girl knows his intentions."

Willy, with anger in his face, wipes the crumbs from his mouth.

"Makes me mad!" he said. "I know Diamond Dick didn't touch that girl. We don't bother them, so why do they bother us?"

"Because they can. When you got no rights, those in charge can do what they want."

"Not for long! When I find them boys—"

"Whatever notions you got yo' head, boy," warned Lela-Ann, "you better think again. They didn't hurt you too much, and they didn't get to Phyllis. You go after them boys, and you gon' get yo'self in a world of trouble. Just leave it alone."

"So, we just got to take it, huh?"

"Boy, when you Colored, you got to take a whole lot in your life. Start learning."

"Yes, ma'am. I better git. Mama might start worrying."

"I'll show you to the door."

Lela-Ann was just showing Willy to the door when the doorbell rang. As Lela-Ann opened it, in walked Gregory with a rifle around his back. He looked upset.

"Good afternoon, Corporal Willborn," Lela-Ann smiled politely.

"No, it's not," said Gregory as he placed his rifle against the wall. "I heard that someone raped Phyllis." He turned to Willy. "Are you Willy?"

"Yes , sir, Corporal Willborn. William Smith. And they didn't rape her; they attacked us. She's not hurt. Just in a pother."

"There's no just about it when someone puts their hands on my woman! But I heard you did right by her, and I thank you." Willy nodded in acknowledgement. Gregory turned to Lela-Ann. "Where's Phyllis?"

"She's upstairs," Lela-Ann answered. Not waiting for permission, he ran up the stairs. He approached the door that was closed and knocked on it.

"Is that you, Lela-Ann?" Mrs. Mitchell asked through the door.

"No ma'am. It's Gregory."

"Gregory?" called Phyllis. "Come in!" When he opened the door, he saw Phyllis in bed and Mrs. Mitchell sitting in a rocking chair. He entered and knelt by his fiancée's side.

"What did they do to you, baby?" he asked, taking her hand.

"They were so disgusting!" Phyllis answered, melancholy, but subdued. "They wanted to—but I'm still a virgin, Gregory. I swear!"

"That doesn't matter, sweetie. I'm so glad you're safe." He embraced Phyllis. "Honey," his eyes became constricted, his nostrils flaring, "Can you remember what they looked like?"

"That just won't do, Gregory Willborn," Mrs. Mitchell spoke up. "You are getting too worked up. I won't have you bringing trouble in this family. I know I speak for Mr. Mitchell when I say let it go. You see she's safe."

"And what about the next woman they go after—the one walking by herself? And what if they did have their way with her? Would you want me to let it go then?"

" 'Vengeance is mine,' saith the Lord."

"Well, maybe the Lord won't mind me helping Him. After all, the police won't do anything about it!"

"I will not argue with you. I'm am just going to say that if you want to marry our daughter, you will put this to rest. Understand?"

"Yes, Mother," Gregory sighed deeply.

"Go on downstairs; Phyllis needs to rest before dinner."

"Yes, Mother," he headed towards the door.

"And Gregory?" Gregory turned back.

"Yes?"

"You called me Mother," she smiled.

"I know," he smiled back, exiting.

Chapter 4:
To the Defense

At 4:00, Mr. Mitchell was still at the bank. He had just gotten off the phone with Mrs. Mitchell. Though he was upset, he was able to maintain restraint in manner and speech. He wanted to go straight home, but he was concerned because of the growing mob his customers told him about. Mr. Daniels, the third partner of the bank, came to his desk.

"Let's just close up, Clarence," he said. "The tellers are starting to get scared because of that mob at the courthouse."

"Very well," sighed Mr. Mitchell. "But I am going to call Mr. Gurley and Dr. Jackson. We need to talk to the sheriff before things get out of hand."

"Are you sure he is going to listen to you?"

"I am confident of it. Sheriff McCullough is a decent man— the most decent White lawman I have known. He will listen to reason."

"If you say so." Mr. Daniels walked away. Mr. Mitchell rose to his feet, walked over to the wall phone, and wound its lever.

"Operator," he said, "get me O.W. Gurley, please. "

Within 20 minutes, Mr. Mitchell, Dr. A.C. Jackson, O.W. Gurley, and other prominent members of the Greenwood community, congregated at the entrance of the sheriff's office.

"So, we're agreed," said Mr. Gurley. "Our objective is to keep Dick Rowland safe—not to release him."

"After all," added Mr. Mitchell, "if we go in there demanding his release, McCullough won't give us the time of day."

"This is still absurd, him being arrested," another man spoke. "That boy wouldn't hurt a mouse crawling into his house."

"That's irrelevant!" Mr. Mitchell asserted. "That mob does not care about innocence. They care about blood: Negro blood! Let's assure his safety today and worry about innocence tomorrow." All of the men nod in agreement. They entered the sheriff's office.

"What do you boys want?" asked an officer at the front desk.

"May we speak to the sheriff?" asked Mr. Gurley.

"Wait here." The deputy walked to the office in the back of the room while the men waited patiently. Minutes later, he returned to the desk with the Sheriff.

"Hello, gentlemen," the sheriff smiled. "What can I do for you?"

"Sheriff McCullough," began Mr. Gurley, "There has been a mob of angry White men gathering at the courthouse, set off by that article in this afternoon's Tribune. They are getting more livid by the minute."

"Yes, I have seen them starting to grow," responded Sheriff McCullough, "And I am fixing to go down there to send them home."

"Sir," interjected Mr. Mitchell. "I know we needn't remind you of the Roy Belton incident last year. A lot of people in Greenwood are becoming worried because if an angry mob is capable of lynching a White man, imagine what they would do to a Colored boy."

"You can tell the residents of Greenwood that they and I are on the same level. I am determined to prevent another Roy Belton incident. I assure you; there will be no lynching. I am planning to sneak him out of jail to make sure he has his day in court."

A White attorney, friends with Mr. Mitchell and Dr. Jackson, had come into the room and heard the exchange.

"Willard," he joined the discussion. "Now, you know that boy's innocent. Why don't you let him go?"

"And you know I can't do that! Even if I thought he was innocent, that girl, Sarah Page, pressed charges, and there are folks who heard her scream and him running out of that Drexel building like he stole something. He wouldn't make it one block with that crazy mob out there. Even if he escaped, the mob would probably go after his family. The best I can go is spirit him out of Tulsa where he'll be safe. And that's what I aim to do. Excuse me, gentlemen." Sheriff McCullough put on his hat and walked around the desk, leaving the building.

"That damned fool, Jones!" shouted the attorney. "I ought to get the DA to arrest him for inciting a riot." He walked away.

"Gentlemen," Mr. Gurley turned to his entourage. "I am assured we can trust Sheriff McCullough. He has just as much to lose if that mob gets out of hand."

"I agree," Dr. Jackson spoke up. "He's nothing like the hotheads I've seen."

"All we need to do now," Mr. Mitchell declared, "Is try to calm our own people down."

"Very true," said Mr. Gurley. "But, I wonder if they trust the Sheriff as much as we do."

"They trust us," said Mr. Mitchell. "That's a start, isn't it?"

"We'll see," answered another man of the entourage. "Let's go."

As Mr. Mitchell began walking home, the phone rang at the Mitchell house.

"Mitchell residence," Lela-Ann answered the phone.

"Good afternoon, this is Sergeant Keith Fowler of the United States Army. Is Corporal Gregory Willborn at your home?"

"He sure is, Sergeant."

"(loud exhaling) Thank the Lord! Could you please have him come to the phone? It's very important."

"Right away, Sergeant." She placed the phone receiver on its stand and walked to the parlor where Gregory was drinking sweet tea on the sofa. "Corporal, a Sergeant Fowler is on the phone for you."

"Sergeant Fowler?" inquired Gregory, setting down his glass, standing up, and walking to the phone with Lela-Ann. "It must be serious. And, Lela-Ann, don't you think it's time to call me Gregory?"

"If that's what you want, Gregory," she smiled as he picked up the phone, walking away.

"Corporal Gregory Willborn," he answered the phone.

"Willborn, do you know what your squad is up to? About 5 of them left base at knock off together, and I hear tell of a group of local veterans getting together to plan the defense of the courthouse. Didn't I tell all of you not to get involved?"

"Sir, I'm just hearing about this myself. I had nothing to do with them walking off. Did they take their rifles?"

"I would have stopped them if they did. If they are armed, it's with pistols."

"With all those White men, madder than a nest of hornets?"

"Willborn, I need your eyes on that courthouse. Get down there, and if you see them, tell them I said to get back to base in one hour, or I will personally recommend their court marshal."

"Do I really need to go after them, sir? I have a bit of a family situation--"

"Willborn, you'll have the rest of your life to tangle with your woman. Get your ass down to that courthouse now! Is that clear?"

"Yes, sir!"

Sergeant Fowler hung up, and Gregory returned the receiver to the transmitter. Frustrated, he collected his rifle, swinging it over his shoulder. Lela-Ann returned to the hallway just as Gregory was donning his military hat.

"Lela-Ann, could you please let the family know I will be back in about an hour? There's something I must attend to."

"Certainly, Gregory. Dinner should be ready by then."

"Sounds good, thanks." He left the house.

As Gregory approached the courthouse downtown, he felt a knot grow in his stomach when he saw the angry mob of White men yelling at the Sheriff and his men as they calmly tried talking to them.

"Bring that nigger out here!" yelled a portly blond man with a thick mustache.

"Yeah, we gonna teach him a lesson!" answered a man in his fifties with rotting teeth, proudly holding a noose he made.

"Look here, folks," answered Sheriff McCullough. "There's not gonna be no lynching here in Tulsa, ya hear? That boy's gonna get his day in court."

"Have you turned nigger lover against us?" a voice yelled from the crowd. "What if it happened to your daughter? Or your wife?"

"I'm telling you to clear out! Rowland is gonna get his justice right!

"Then give him to us!" yelled a young man. "We'll give him justice!"

As Gregory watched this spectacle, he noticed a group of Colored veterans from the Great War march confidently into the area. Far behind them walked the five men from his unit. He firmly walked over to them and stopped them in their tracks.

"What are you men doing here?" he demanded.

"We gotta keep them from lynching Rowland like they itching to do!" answered one of the privates.

"And just forget the sergeant's orders, right?"

"He'll understand; he knows the color of his skin," another private spoke up.

"Understand this! As sure as he knows his skin is black, he is trying to save it and yours! He told me to tell you that if you fools aren't back at base in 30 minutes, he will personally make sure each of you are court marshaled."

"But Corporal--" protested the first private.

"No buts! Return to base on the double!"

"Yes, sir," the men replied, turning back from where they came. He watched his soldiers depart, and then he turned to see the veterans approach the Sheriff.

"What do you boys want?" asked the Sheriff. "You can't go in the courthouse; it's on lockdown."

"No, sir," responded the leader of the veterans. "We don't want to go in. It looks like you need some help. We wants to help you keep them from getting Dick Rowland."

"You a good man for protecting Rowland," another veteran added. "but while that there mob is still mad as dogs, they can charge in this courthouse at anytime."

"I thank you for coming out here like this," answered Sheriff McCullough, "but I think we'll be fine without your help. No one tried to get through yet, so they're hearing me out."

"Now, Sheriff," insisted another veteran, "They got that Belton boy last year, and he was White. You know they'll do more than just hang Rowland; you know that!"

"Boys, I told you I don't need help! Besides, that was a different sheriff. Maybe he wasn't up to the task, but I am. There ain't gonna be no more lynchings in Tulsa! Not while I'm Sheriff."

"If you say so, boss," another veteran said reluctantly.

"And I'll need you to clear out now. I've got this under control."

"Come on," the leader instructed his men. They turned and left.

"What did those coons think they were going to do?" speculated a smartly dressed member of the mob, wearing a straw boater hat.

"Niggers with guns." another man fumed. "That's a dangerous sight." He and other members started to leave the area, and Gregory snuck away before he could be noticed.

As Gregory entered the Mitchell house, Mr. Mitchell entered the hallway as Gregory was removing his rifle from his shoulder, returning it to the same corner as before.

"Where were you, son?" Mr. Mitchell asked.

"There was word that a few men from my outfit were headed to the courthouse, so my sergeant ordered me to go and send them back to base."

"That was swift thinking on the sergeant's part. Soldiers must not get themselves involved in civilian affairs. They would not be able to help much anyway. Besides, a few community leaders and I talked to the Sheriff. He promised to do his part to secret Rowland out of jail so that the mob wouldn't get him."

"You honestly believe him, sir?"

"Don't sell him short, my boy. He is not like the last sheriffs. He appreciates what we are trying to accomplish here. He knows that we only want to keep to ourselves and live in peace."

"I don't know, Papa. He'll need more than that police force if those men don't go home. He'll need the military."

"Let's hope it doesn't come to that," said Mr. Mitchell.

Suddenly, Phyllis appeared from the top of the stairs and came down, dressed for dinner.

"Phillybug," called Mr. Mitchell, "You've had a difficult day. You should have stayed in bed. Lela-Ann could have brought up a tray for you."

"I'm fine, Papa," answered Phyllis. "Besides, I didn't want to lay in bed while Gregory is here, and Mama says that it's not proper for a man to spend too much time in a woman's bedroom."

"Your Mama's right," answered Mr. Mitchell. "I'm just glad you weren't hurt. I should pay a visit to Willy to give him my thanks. "

"You look grand tonight," Gregory said to his woman.

"So do you," beamed Phyllis. As Mrs. Mitchell and Lela-Ann exited the kitchen, holding platters of food, the three of them walking into the dining room, with Gregory and Phyllis holding hands.

"Gregory," Mr. Mitchell spoke as he forked his pot roast a few minutes later, "I think you had better stay here and sleep in Junior's room. It might be dangerous walking around at night with all that is transpiring. We go to bed at 10 o'clock."

"As long as it won't be too much trouble, Papa," answered Gregory.

"What trouble? You are going to be living here soon!"

"Thank you. Things are really getting out of hand out there. And those veterans showing up the way they did, I don't know if that made things better or worse."

"Some of the men left the courthouse, didn't they?" asked Mrs. Mitchell.

"They did, but they were all puffed up about Colored men with guns."

"Perhaps it is for the best that the Sheriff declined their help," said Mr. Mitchell. "A group of Colored veterans pointing guns at White men just might make them angrier."

"It's funny, though," said Gregory. "They drafted the most of us to fight this country's war, but they are offended to see us in uniform or holding a gun."

"It's not as complicated as you think, son. My daddy chopped sugarcane using a cane knife as soon as he was old enough to hold it in his hand. He used it at every harvest and would get a lash or two for not working fast enough. You may ask, why didn't he ever use that knife to kill the overseer or even the master? That knife is sharp enough to kill them instantly after all. There are two reasons why he did not take that tool that built his master's wealth and put him in his grave. First, he knew that he would never escape. Second, he never thought about it because the master and every White man he knew took away his ability to think for himself. Third, and more importantly, he never gave up hope that something better would come his way. His life taught me to take my life in my own hands and use my strengths to enrich my community that will thank me for it and not to make richer those who won't let me drink a cup of coffee in their restaurants or sit where I want on their streetcars."

"Thank God for you and your daddy!" exclaimed Lela-Ann, as she enjoyed her dinner at the table with the family.

"Amen to that!" responded Mrs. Mitchell. "Well, let's try to talk about something more cheerful, shall we? Gregory, how goes the search for a room?"

"Slowly, but surely," answered Gregory. "Ms. Jones says that she might have an opening next week on the second floor. It is right on Greenwood Avenue."

"That's nice. What about lodgings in one of the Gurley buildings?"

"Gurley doesn't have any openings right now."

"I'll have a talk with O.W. when the Rowland business settles down," announced Mr. Mitchell. "I'm sure he can find something for you."

"No need to go through any trouble, Papa."

"There's no trouble, son. Let's have no more of that!"

"So, you know the O.W. Gurley?"

"Papa knows all the important men of this town," Phyllis joined the conversation. "Before I forget, your favorite color is maroon, isn't it?"

"It sure is, Lissy!" he kissed her on the cheek.

"And linen is a suitable fabric for a bachelor, so I'll need to pick up some maroon linen fabric this week."

"Phyllis is making some curtains for your room," Mrs. Mitchell proudly clarified.

"That is so keen!" he smiled at Phyllis.

"Anything for you," Phyllis answered him as they leaned towards each other, sharing a quick and soft kiss.

"Not at the table, you too," said Mrs. Mitchell.

"Is that so?" asked Mr. Mitchell with a sly grin as he kissed Mrs. Mitchell equally quickly and softly.

"Well, I declare!" exclaimed Mrs. Mitchell. "You are as bad as they are!"

After the family enjoyed their dinner together, Lela-Ann cleared the table and washed the dishes whilst the rest of the family adjourned to the parlor for the rest of the evening. Mr. Mitchell read the Bible silently in his chair whilst Mrs. Mitchell played church music on the piano, reflectively. Phyllis and Gregory sat together on the sofa, holding hands as they listened to Mrs. Mitchell's playing. When the grandfather clock struck 10 o'clock, Mr. Mitchell put down his Bible and rose to his feet as Mrs. Mitchell ended her rendition.

"Well, it's time for bed everyone. Tomorrow will be a busy day, so we will need our rest. "

"Phyllis," Mrs. Mitchell also stood up, "you may bid Gregory good night." Both Gregory and Phyllis rose from the sofa.

"Good night, Gregory," she smiled, squeezing his hand.

"Good night, Lissy," he smiled back. She reluctantly released his hand. "And good night to you too, Mama. Papa."

"Good night son," Mr. Mitchell pat Gregory's arm and left the parlor, climbing the stairs.

"Sleep well," said Mrs. Mitchell, following her husband with Phyllis at her side.

"When you ready," Lela-Ann said to Gregory, "I'll show you where you gon' sleep."

"I'm ready now, Lela-Ann," Gregory answered.

"It's right upstairs. Follow me."

Lela-Ann led Gregory out of the parlor and up the stairs to the bedrooms. He was halfway up the stairs when the doorbell rang.

"Callers at his hour!" huffed an annoyed Lela-Ann. "I tell you, some folks ain't got the sense they was born with!"

"I'll get it," said Gregory. Once he reached the bottom of the stairs, he peered out the window as he approached the door. "Wait a minute; I think it's Willy."

"What would that boy want this hour?" asked Lela-Ann, also descending the stairs.

"I'll ask." Gregory opened the door, and it indeed was Willy, a distressed look on his face. "Willy, what's wrong?"

"Them crackers are back at the courthouse!" shouted Willy.

"What! I thought the Sheriff had this under control."

"He don't. About a thousand of them came back--this time with guns. Thousands more came too. They all over the courthouse, Corporal!"

"Lord God!" exclaimed Lela-Ann. "They gon' lynch that boy for sho!"

"Not if I can help it!" said Willy, much braver than earlier.

"What are you talking about, Willy?" asked Gregory. He then looked down at Willy's right hand and saw him holding a pistol. Willy nodded his head.

"Like I said: not if I can help it."

"Man, what are you fixing to do with that gun?"

"Corporal, it's not just me, and it's not just those Colored men at the courthouse earlier. We organized. We found as many men with guns as we could find, and we are going down to that courthouse to make sure none of them 'good old boys' get their filthy hands on Rowland. We need you, though. We heard what you did in the War, and we know you a crack shot. We need your help, sir."

Before Gregory could respond, he heard voices of dozens of men walking down the street. He then saw a group of men with rifles and shotguns walking past the house. All of the men were headed in the direction of downtown.

"You see, Corporal?" Willy said proudly. "We are going down to defend that courthouse now. We protect our own."

Gregory buttoned up his military jacket with determination.

"Let me get my rifle," said Gregory, heading towards Mr. Mitchell's study.

"I knew you were with us!" Willy grinned. Lela-Ann, apprehensive, yanked Gregory's arm.

"Boy, are you crazy? You can't go out there and get killed."

"I won't get killed," Gregory assured her. "This is just another battle."

"Even if them White men don't kill you, Mr. Mitchell will!"

"Well then," smiled Gregory, grabbing his rifle, "It's a good night to die."

"That ain't funny, boy!" Lela-Ann slapped his arm.

"Wasn't meant to be, Lela-Ann."

"Stubborn as a mule! Yeah, you gon' fit into this family real fine!"

"Don't worry, Lela-Ann," he put his arm on her shoulder reassuringly. "I'll come back in one piece."

"You'd better! But what'll I tell the family?"

"That I'll be back before breakfast."

"Come on, Corporal," said Willy, inching towards the door. "Got my daddy's car right outside."

"See you soon," Gregory kissed Lela-Ann on the cheek before rushing out the door with Willy.

When Willy drove through downtown Tulsa, it was mostly deserted, but he could hear the same yelling that he heard earlier in the day, but only amplified. They were a block away from the courthouse when they saw a large group of Colored men with guns marching towards it.

"Pull over here, Willy," said Gregory. "I don't think we can get any closer." Willy pulled over without questioning, and they both exited the car. "Are you sure you are up to this, Willy?"

"Corporal, " Willy answered, "I was ready since those crackers went after your fiancée this afternoon. I ain't turning back."

"Good, because once we get out there, you are a soldier."

"Yes, sir!"

"Let's go then."

     Both Gregory and Willy joined the throng of armed Colored men marching towards the courthouse. Some acknowledged old friends and others introduced each other and mentioned the branches of military and battalions in which they served. All of them were proud men. Proud of their community. Proud of their accomplishments. Proud of their heritage. They were determined to protect their own and all they worked for.

     As the large group of veterans and men approached the courthouse steps, the angry mob grew incredibly restless and yelled louder. Gregory and Willy were amongst the last group of the men. As both men saw the angry, gun-wielding crowd, Gregory swallowed hard while Willy began to perspire. When he fought in Germany, he faced men who were conscripted to fight for their countries and would rather be home. This time, the men he was facing hated him passionately. It did not matter that he fought for America, nor did it matter that he was an American by birth and citizenship. To him, the enemy he faced was far more lethal than German soldiers.

"Sheriff," said one of the men, as he climbed the steps, "You have a problem."

"You said it, boy," said Sheriff McCullough, exasperated and exhausted. "Now, I told y'all to clear out. I also told y'all I don't need no help."

"Now, Sheriff," the presumed leader was more persistent, "You told us earlier that you didn't need help, but there weren't as many of these crazy men out here as there are now. And a lot of them have guns now. Now, something is gonna happen if you don't make them leave and leave soon. There's already talk in Greenwood that this here mob already stormed the jail. We are gonna help you protect this courthouse and Rowland."

"I respect your bravery and dedication to your people. Still, you've got nothing to worry about. Dick Rowland is safe, and he's gonna stay that way. These men out here are just angry and riled up, but none of them got past me yet. Chief Gustafson talked to them, and so did the Reverend from the Presbyterian church out yonder. It's getting late, so they'll get tired and go home. And I am going to tell you the same thing I told them: go home. We don't need any help."

The leader walked towards the men he came with and began to speak to them on what to do. The decision was made; they would obey the Sheriff and go home, but they would keep watch, and a few men would stay nearby for reconnaissance. Reluctantly, the armed men began walking away.

The White mob, however, became increasingly incensed at their presence. They began to berate the Colored force.

"Maybe we oughta string up some more coons tonight!" threatened a man in his early twenties.

"What the hell is that nigger-loving Sheriff thinking?" fumed an old man. "He should be arresting them animals for threatening to shoot White men!"

Another man began to approach a tall Colored veteran.

"Hey, boy! Hey!" he yelled at him. The veteran turned to look at him. "Where you going with that gun, nigger?"

"I'm going to use it if I have to," the veteran answered, looking at him with intent.

"Like hell you are!" insisted the angry White man. "Give it to me!" He tried to wrestle the rifle out of the veteran's hands, but the veteran used it to shove him away. The men began to wrestle the weapon away from each other. The veteran, being stronger and with military training, succeeded in knocking the hate-filled bigot to the ground.

Then, like a knell, a shot from a gun rang in everyone's ears.

As if on instinct, the White ruffians opened fire on the Colored force, and the latter responded in kind. The whole city of Tulsa was awakened by the loud gunshots that sounded like firecrackers of the 4th of July events to come.

"We are we gon' do?" shouted Willy to Gregory as they were shooting their guns at the mob.

"Just keep shooting!" Gregory shouted back. "When I say so, we are going to make our way to the car and get the hell out of here!"

As everyone kept shooting at everyone else, a growing cloud of smoke enveloped both sides, making it difficult for everyone to see everyone else in the darkness.

After what seemed like an eternity, all of Colored men knew their defense was becoming increasingly futile.

"Pull back!" yelled one of the men. "Pull back!"

"Now, Willy!" shouted Gregory. "Start running; I'll cover you!" Both men retreated from the courthouse area quickly. As Willy ran, Gregory followed behind to protect him. By this time, more and more men were retreating the area, getting into their cars or running on foot, heading towards Greenwood. Once they reached the car, Willy hurried inside and started the engine. Gregory approaching the car and before entering, he looked around. A White man from the mob approached from the cloud of smoke.

"Go to hell, nigger!" he screamed, raising a pistol. Without hesitating, Gregory promptly shot the man through the forehead, killing him instantly. Looking to see who else was coming, he went over to the man's body and removed the pistol from his hand. He then rushed into the car with Willy, and Willy hit the accelerator, making a U-turn away from the area.

Chapter 5:
Death and Destruction

Back at the Mitchell home, Mr. Mitchell paced back and forth in the front hallway while Mrs. Mitchell, Phyllis, and Lela-Ann sat in the parlor. Except for Lela-Ann, everyone was in their bedclothes and robes.

"Violet, I should strangle that boy!" Mr. Mitchell raised his voice. "I thought he knew better than to go pick fights."

"Papa," Phyllis weighed in, "Gregory does not pick fights. He believes in honor, not brawling. If he went with Willy to the courthouse, it was for a good reason."

"Now, Phillybug, there was no reason for him to go down there at all. We already spoke to the Sheriff, and he promised to keep Rowland safe from any lynching."

"For heaven's sake, Clarence," said Mrs. Mitchell, "Try to be realistic. If thousands of White men decide to push McCullough aside and go inside the courthouse, what can he and a handful of deputies do? Maybe with trained, disciplined veterans, they will think twice about trying to get into the courthouse. Maybe they will go home."

"Violet, " countered Mr. Mitchell, "Do you honestly think the Sheriff will let them stand guard at the courthouse?"

Before Mrs. Mitchell could answer, they were interrupted by the faint gunfire from the courthouse downtown.

"Papa," asked Phyllis, "What's that noise? They can't be shooting off firecrackers. It's not even July."

"Honey," Lela-Ann joined the conversation, "Them ain't firecrackers."

"They most certainly are not!" exclaimed Mr. Mitchell. "Those are gunshots!"

"Oh, my Lord," lamented Mrs. Mitchell. "Clarence, please tell me those shots are not from the courthouse."

"My dear, if you must ask, you already know the answer."

"Gregory!" cried Phyllis. "Please be all right. Please come back!"

"Now, now," Mr. Mitchell wrapped an arm around Phyllis to comfort her. "Your Gregory is brave and quick. He knows how to get himself out of this. But, Violet, I'm starting to get a bad feeling. I want you and Phyllis to go up and get dressed. Pack a few things, only what you need. You too, Lela-Ann. I should hurry and pack some things also."

"Why, Clarence?" asked Mrs. Mitchell. "What do you think is going to happen?"

"I'm not sure, but I want us to be prepared for anything. Don't forget Red Summer." Mrs. Mitchell gasped. "Yes, so no more discussion. Let's get dressed."

    While Lela-Ann rushed to her room behind the kitchen, The Mitchells hurried to their rooms to dress and pack. Just as Mr. Mitchell finished dressing, the doorbell rang. He went to his closet and retrieved his shotgun. He turned to Violet as he left the bedroom.

"Just keep packing," he told her. As he headed for the stairs in the hallway, he stood by Phyllis' door. "Keep dressing and packing!"

"Yes, Papa," she answered through the door. As he descended the stairs, he heard Lela-Ann walking into the foyer.

"I'll answer it, Lela-Ann! Return to your room and finish packing!"

"Yes, Mr. Mitchell," she said, turning back around towards the kitchen.

Once Mr. Mitchell reached the bottom of the stairs, he held his gun vertically, walked to the side of the door, and peered through the window. When he saw Gregory and Willy, he lowered his gun and opened the door.

"They comin'!" shouted Willy as both men hurried inside.

"What the devil happened!" Mr. Mitchell demanded.

"Papa," Gregory struggled to catch his breath, "Those crackers are going mad dog crazy! The Sheriff told us to go home and that he didn't need the help we wanted to give him, but as we tried to leave, they started hounding us. Someone's gun fired, and then we started shooting at each other. We started to retreat, but now they are headed towards Greenwood!"

"Violet, Lela-Ann, Phyllis, get down here!" yelled Mr. Mitchell. As if on cue, all three women came from their bedrooms and into the parlor, fully dressed and carrying sacks.

"Gregory!" Phyllis embraced her betrothed. She looked up at him happily, but her face dropped when she saw his distressed disposition.

"Clarence," Mrs. Mitchell spoke up, "What's the matter?"

"There was a shoot-out at the courthouse, and the Whites are on their way to Greenwood."

"What?!" exclaimed Mrs. Mitchell and Lela-Ann.

"You heard me. You womenfolk need to leave now." He reached into his jacket pocket and retrieved a key, handing it to Mrs. Mitchell. "Take the Brisco. Drive north from here and don't stop for anyone." He paused to look at Phyllis and Lela-Ann. "I need you two to keep your heads down at all times, especially when there are people about. Mrs. Mitchell can pass, but you two can't. Whatever you do, once you leave Tulsa, keep going!"

"Drive to Owasso," added Gregory. "Go to my parents' house. It's a white-painted two story brick colonial. Take Main Street to the town hall and turn left. Drive about half a mile until you get to the Colored section. You will see it."

"But what about you?" Mrs. Mitchell asked her husband.

"I'll come for you when this is over," he answered.

"Papa, come with us!" cried Phyllis.

"I've got to stay here and protect the house."

"Papa, no!"

"Clarence, forget the house!" insisted Mrs. Mitchell. "You mean more to us than any house!"

"This is our home, darling," he said. "This is our land, and I have worked hard all of my life to provide a home for us, and its ours; we pay taxes for it. I am not about to let lecherous heathens take it away from us. I'm staying."

"I'm staying too," announced Gregory.

"Me too," added Willy. Mr. Mitchell smiled and nodded at them to show his appreciation.

"Then, let me stay too, Papa!" sobbed Phyllis. "Let me help you!"

Gregory gathered Phyllis in his arms and kissed her with all the passion he could muster. Phyllis wrapped her arms around his neck in reciprocation.

"You could help us so much by getting out of here right now before these bastards get here," he told her tenderly. "You will see me soon. I am not going to die here, and neither is your father. I love you so much, girl."

"I love you too, Gregory," Phyllis replied, soothed.

"We must go now, Phyllis," Mrs. Mitchell grabbed Phyllis' arm, pulling her away from Gregory.

"Wait," said Gregory to the women. He reached into his pockets and retrieved two revolvers, the smaller one from the man he shot. He handed one gun to Phyllis and the other to Mrs. Mitchell. "Just in case. You know how to use these?"

Both women nodded their heads.

"Good. You probably won't need to use them if you keep driving, but just in case."

"Now, ladies," said Mr. Mitchell, "You really need to get going. " He led them to the front door and opened it for them. Mrs. Mitchell, tears streaming down her face, quickly embraced her husband.

"Clarence," she spoke. "Promise me one thing. Promise me you won't take any unnecessary risks."

"I promise, Violet," Mr. Mitchell squeezed her tight.

Once he released her, she grasped Phyllis' hand and walked out the door, Lela-Ann close behind. Even in tears, Violet held her head up as she lead her crying daughter and stunned maid to their vehicle. As the car drove onto the street, Phyllis and Lela-Ann waved to their men. The men waved back as the women drove speedily away.

"Mr. Mitchell," Gregory turned to his future father-in-law, "I sure hope you've got enough ammunition." The three men turned and went inside, closing the door.

"I have plenty from when we moved to this state," said Mr. Mitchell. "Until now, I never needed to use it. Come on upstairs."

They began walking up the stairs and into the master bedroom. He went to his closet and dragged out a chest, and placed it on the bed. He then removed two semi-automatic pistols and a rifle. He also removed two felt sacks, giving one to Gregory. Gregory looked into the sack, took out a bullet, and studied its caliber.

"This'll fit," he said, replacing the bullet.

"I'm sure it will," said Mr. Mitchell. "I have ammunition for rifles, shotguns, and pistols. Buckshot for the shotgun and hollow-point exploding rounds for everything else. Even if the bullets don't kill them, they'll do enough damage to stop them. Willy, go around the house, collect all the lamps and lanterns, and bring them up here."

"Yes, sir," said Willy, turning quickly to his task.

"Now, boy," Mr. Mitchell turned to Gregory, "What trouble have you brought to this house?"

"I have done no such thing," answered Gregory, taken aback. "I told you what happened. Willy and I stayed in the back of the group. When the Sheriff told us to leave, we obliged him. It was those crackers who stopped us. I don't know who fired, but it wasn't me, and it wasn't Willy. This was going to happen either way, sir. If we weren't at the back, we wouldn't have gotten away as quickly as we did, and all of you would have been in danger."

"But son, what were you thinking?"

"I was thinking of Laura Nelson and her son hanging off a bridge. I was thinking about my men risking their lives for this damned country and being treated like less than men when they came home. I was thinking about those two White boys and what they would have done to Phyllis if there were no men around. I was thinking that even a resident of glorious Greenwood was going to be another lynched brother. Papa, that's what I was thinking. Aren't you sick of all this?"

"Yes, I am sick of it, boy! But what can we do? We are living in their country!"

"Their country is on Indian land! They did not bring us here to be a part of it; they brought us here to do their work for them!"

"But what can we do about it! Nothing! Just live our lives and prove them wrong. At least we have our own communities. Look at we have! Look what we can do!"

"You know, Papa? Maybe that Jamaican, Marcus Garvey, was right. Maybe our place is in Africa."

"Maybe it's not! We are not African; we are Americans. Colored, but American!"

Gregory walked over to the window. In the brief silence, there was the growing sound of yelling, gunshots, and people screaming and groaning.

"Listen to that!" he pointed to the window. "Does it sound like they care we are Americans?"

Before Mr. Mitchell could answer, Willy entered the room as briskly as he left. He was carrying a box teeming with lamps and lanterns.

"They comin', y'all!" he said, catching his breath.

"Gregory, go downstairs and turn off all the lights," Mr. Mitchell ordered. "Barricade the back door."

"I'm on it," said Gregory, hurrying away. Mr. Mitchell held out his arms for the box.

"Let me have that, son." Willy gave him the box.

He then commenced removing the glass chimney from each lamp, setting them to the side. He removed a lantern from the box, raised its glass, and lit the wick with his lighter. He then placed the lantern on his wife's vanity.

"Cut the light off," he told Willy. Willy nodded his head and pressed the light button. The room went dark, with the only available light coming from the lantern.

"Mr. Mitchell?" Willy asked. "If I may, what do you need them lamps for?"

"Willy, I don't know how much you know about war, but there is something called a hand grenade that a soldier can use to take out more than one enemy at a time. We don't have hand grenades, unfortunately, but this is the next best thing. We light each wick, and we throw it at them when needed. "

"I understand. And sir, don't be mad at Gregory. Going to the courthouse was my idea. "

"I know you did what you had to do," answered Mr. Mitchell. "We'll talk about it later."

Suddenly, they heard a crashing sound from next door. Willy looked outside, and he saw two White men standing outside of a neighbor's house. They had just broken a window next to the door.

"Come on out of there!" they yelled. Gregory came back into the room.

"Mr. and Mrs. Langston," Mr. Mitchell shook his head, clasping his shotgun.

"Get out the window, Willy!" whispered Gregory. Willy veered to the side, looking intently outside.

"You better come out," warned one of the men outside, holding a can of kerosene, "or we'll burn you out!"

Suddenly, an old man in a nightshirt and an old woman wearing a robe and a cotton night bonnet, Mr. and Mrs. Langston, came slowly outside with their hands up.

"Please don't shoot us," pleaded the Mr. Langston. "Please! I don't even know what this is about. We are just old people; we don't mean trouble to anybody."

"We just wanna talk to you, Uncle," the younger White man grinned. "Let us take you for a drive, and we won't bother Auntie or your house. I give you my word."

"All right," said Mr. Langston, lowering his arms.

"First," said the older White man, removing a noose from his car, "Let's put this on you."

"What?!" shouted Mr. Langston, horrified.

"Well, how else are we gonna drag ya?"

"No!" shouted Mrs. Langston, bursting into tears. "He didn't do nothing!"

"You be quiet now!" demanded the younger White man, pointing his gun at Mrs. Langton.

"Lucille, " Mr. Langston turned to his wife, "it's all right. Don't argue with these boys. I love you, woman." Mr.

Langston turned back to the older White man. "So, you want to drag an old man? Come on, then."

"Get his hands," the older White man told the younger man.

"You stay there," the younger man warned Mrs. Langston, lowering his pistol. He walked back over to Mr. Langston. "We ain't got nothin' personal 'gainst ya, Uncle. This is a lesson to coon bastards who want to rape White women and shoot at White men." The older man proceeded to place the noose over Mr. Langston's neck.

"Oh, God, no!" sobbed Mrs. Langston, collapsing to the ground.

"May God forgive y'all," said Mr. Langston as the men tightened the noose around his neck.

"We don't need God's forgiveness, boy," sneered the older man. "We are doing His work. Harlan, watch him. I've gotta tie the other end to the truck."

"He ain't goin' nowheres," answered the younger man.

As the older man grabbed the other end of the rope, he only took two steps before there was a loud cracking sound and he was shot through the forehead. As blood oozed from his skull and a stunned look on his face, the man fell backwards--dead.

The younger man, shocked, stepped into the middle of the street and surveyed the area. He then looked back at his partner's body and followed the trail into the second floor of the Mitchell home. With fury, he fired a shot towards the respective window, but it only hit a brick. Livid, he aimed his gun at the window again, but before firing, a bullet struck him through the throat, causing him to collapse, his body falling on Mr. Langston's feet. Back in the master bedroom of the Mitchell home, smoke whirled out of Gregory's rifle.

"Told you the Corporal is a crack shot!" Willy smiled.

"Willy," answered Gregory, still looking out the window with his rifle. "I need you to go out and get whatever weapons they have. I'll cover you. Give the old man a gun and tell him to take his wife and get the hell out of town."

"Yes, sir," said Willy, heading for the door.

"And Willy!"

"Yeah?" Willy stopped.

"Don't take any more time out there than you need."

"Yes, sir." He proceeded to race down the stairs and out the door. Upon reaching the street, he saw the old man still standing there with rope around his neck, in shock. Willy went over and gently loosened the noose, removing it from around his neck. He took the pistol out of the younger man's dead hand, giving it to Mr. Langston. Still in shock, he accepted the weapon. His wife ran over and embraced her husband.

"Otis! Otis! Oh, Otis!" she loudly sobbed into his chest. Mr. Langston finally composed himself to comfort his wife as Willy somberly removed a pistol from the dead older man's pocket and confiscated an ammunition pouch from the car they came in. He then walked back over to the elderly couple.

"Y'all got a car?" he asked them.

"In the carport," Mr. Langston answered.

"Good. Get in and get going. Stop for nobody, hear?"

"God bless you, son!" said Mr. Langston.

"Corporal Willborn is the one who saved y'all, not me."

"Well, I hope we meet again so I can thank you both properly. Come on, Lucille. If we don't leave now, God may not spare us next time." He led his wife towards their carport. Willy watched as they boarded their Model T.

"Thank you so much!" said Mrs. Langston, still sobbing, as they drove away.

Willy then checked his surroundings and returned to the house.

"Two pistols and a bag of ammunition," he announced to the other men. "That's all they had."

"Better than nothing," said Mr. Mitchell. "This is only the beginning."

"We'll just grab the ammunition of those we kill," responded Gregory. "Willy and I can take turns. Only when it's safe though. We must be cautious of any traps. "

"What'll we do when we run out of bullets?" asked Willy.

"Don't ask, brother," said Gregory. "Just don't ask."

Suddenly, they heard the sound of gunshots coming from the street. As Mr. Mitchell looked outside the window, he saw a truckload of White men driving down the street, shooting randomly into houses. A Colored man came out of his house with his hands up, his pregnant wife not too far behind. The men guffawed as the truck stopped.

"Willy," commanded Mr. Mitchell, "Light me one of those lamps!" Willy took the lighter Mr. Mitchell held for him and promptly complied.

"Whatcha doin', boy?" one of the White men asked the Colored man, his hands still in the air. "You surrenderin'?"

"Yes, sir," the Colored man answered. "Just let us go, please. We had nothing to do with all this."

"You're probably the first Colored man to surrender tonight, so I'm kinda unprepared. Boys, what you think we should do with these niggers?"

"I got something!" shouted the White man sitting next to the driver.

He pulled out a large pistol and shot the Colored man, blasting off a part of his skull and killing him instantly. His pregnant wife, screaming, began to run from the men. A man in the back of the truck, however, stood up and shot her in the back. She staggered briefly and fell down.

"Hold on, boys," said the driver. "The negress might be dead, but that pickaninny might still be alive."

"Not for long," the third White man responded.

He exited the truck and opened a switchblade, making his intentions clear. He then walked over to the Colored woman's body and was just about to kneel over her when a bullet from Gregory's gun struck his crown. Before the other men in the truck could react, Mr. Mitchell threw the lit lamp at the car. When the makeshift bomb impacted the truck's cab, it immediately immolated it. The men in the truck, also burning, panicked and tried to escape, but they were trapped. The vehicle exploded and was engulfed in flames.

"Bastards!" exclaimed Gregory. "I'm glad we sent the women away when we did. Phyllis couldn't handle this."

"I always hoped she could feel safe in her own home," lamented Mr. Mitchell. "But they won't leave us in peace."

"Peace is a foreign word for them crackers!" added Willy.

"I almost feel safer in the French trenches than here," said Gregory. "Hell, the French loved us!" He turned to Willy. "I appreciate you helping us, and I know it's too late, but you should be with your own family now."

"It's good," Willy answered. "My aunt is with my family, and I got two older brothers, and my daddy is good with a gun, which we got lots of. They'll be fine all right."

"That's good to hear," said Mr. Mitchell. "I'll help your family any way I can after this." He looked outside at Greenwood, watching buildings burn and the fire spreading. "By dawn, all of our businesses will be gone. At least those with money in my bank won't lose much. Everything is kept in the vault before closing. They can burn the bank, but not the vault. As for us, we'll stay here as long as we can. Then we'll need to get the car and make a run for it."

After he finished his sentence, they heard the screech of a car braking.

"Now what?" asked an exasperated Gregory.

They looked outside and saw three men exiting a quadricycle car down the street. One of the men dragged a jug of kerosene from the vehicle while another wrapped a rag around a broken tree branch. He then dipped the torch into the kerosene, and the third man lit it with a match, setting it on fire. The first man threw kerosene onto the corner of a department store. However, as the second man was about to set the store on fire, a panicked White man ran towards them.

"Wait, stop!" He shouted. "Stop! I own that building! It's White-owned!" Then men looked at him up and down, and then continued to approach the building.

"Wait a minute," said Mr. Mitchell. "Why, that's I.J. Buck; he owns a few properties here in Greenwood."

"Trying to save his investments," dryly responded Gregory.

"No, stop!" Mr. Buck yelled at the men, grabbing the arm of the man holding the torch. The man responded by brutally shoving him to the ground.

"Go away, nigger lover!" he threatened him.

"Before we teach you a lesson!" the third man added. Mr. Buck quickly rose to his feet and ran to the intersection as the second man applied the torch to the building, setting it on fire.

"Help, somebody! Help!" he yelled. A police car drove by. "Officer! Officer!" The car stopped, and a policeman exited. "Call the fire department and arrest those men! This is my building."

"Sir, the firemen are all out trying to put out fires."

"At least arrest those arsonists! For God's sake man! Aren't you a lawman?"

"Look around you," said the officer. "We've got too much to do tonight already without trying to save your building. Serves you right for building for Negroes anyway!" He walked back to his car but stopped and faced the three rioters. "You morons get on home! I see you out here again, and I'll haul all of you in!"

"Whatever," said the third man as the three of them returned to their car and drove off. The police officer looked at Mr. Buck, shook his head, and boarded the police car, which drove away. Mr. Buck, distraught, just stood there and watched his property burn.

"This is getting worse," said Mr. Mitchell, watching from the window. They saw many of their neighbors running from their homes and driving away.

Minutes later, a fire truck approached the intersection and stopped in front of the burning department store as the fire began to spread to the adjacent building. Just as the firemen sprung out of their truck, a White rioter ran over to them and fired his shotgun in the air. A large group of rioters, including women, approached them.

"You just get back in your truck and keep driving!" yelled the leader.

"We are on the job, folks," answered one of the firemen. "We need to put out these fires."

"Is your job worth getting shot over?" the leader smiled menacingly at them. "To help a bunch of niggers?"

"Whose side are you on?" shouted a rioter.

"Fine, have it your way," the first fireman answered. They returned to their truck and drove away. The mob then turned onto the street of the Mitchell home.

"They're really coming now!" said Willy.

The mob proceeded to splinter off, group by group. Each group broke open a door to each house, making any remaining residents leave, and then they turned on the lights, rummaging through the residents' belongings. The men watched in horror as they saw men and women exiting the homes with jewelry and other valuables.

"They had a piano in that house," said a woman, wearing pearls that she stole. "You've worked hard all your life, and you could never afford a piano or these pearls!"

"No wonder they think they're better than us!" her husband replied.

"Had fun shopping?" another rioter asked his wife. She smiled and hugged him. She was wearing a mink stole.

"Damn thieves!" fumed Mr. Mitchell. As could be predicted, when a group of rioters left one of the houses across the street, they set the house on fire. The men saw the rioters begin to cross over to their side of the street.

"Get ready!" said Gregory.

"Light me a lamp, Willy," said Mr. Mitchell. Willy complied quickly.

As soon as Mr. Mitchell saw them in the middle of the street, he aimed the lamp at the front of them and threw it. When the lamp crashed onto the street, the flames instantly spread to the rioters, setting many on fire. Most of those who were not aflame retreated the area quickly. A dozen rioters who were unharmed drew their guns and fired on the house, not knowing exactly where to shoot. When they started to approach the house, Mr. Mitchell threw another lit lamp at them, setting some of them on fire.

About eight rioters, unharmed, ran to an unaffected area and began shooting at the window to the master bedroom. This time, the three men returned fire.

"We need to spread out," said Gregory. "Papa, I need you to go to Phyllis' room."

"Good idea," said Mr. Mitchell. "As he turned to the door, he felt a sharp, burning pain in his upper arm, as if he had been seared by a red hot coal. He shouted in pain.

"Are you okay?" Gregory asked.

"They just grazed my arm," he said. "I'm fine." He retreated to Phyllis' room and continued defending the house.

For what seemed like a decade, the three men engaged in a gun battle between the four rioters while the houses across the street were burning. It seemed as if they were firing into the air at first, but then Willy shot a man through his side. One of the men dragged the injured man to safety while the other two continued firing.

Both men stopped shooting when they heard the sound of a gun cocking behind them.

"Hold it right there, boys!" they heard a man say. "Now, drop the guns, and turn around real slow. Any sudden moves, and I'll send you black animals to hell right now!"

Both Gregory and Willy unreservedly obliged him. The turned around to face a bearded, gruff-looking White man wearing a wide-brimmed hat. He was pointing a .357 Magnum at them.

"That's right," he continued. "You boys forgot to board up the windows. I couldn't break down the back door, so I got in through the kitchen window. I left something cooking in there. Hope you don't mind. Tell you what we're gonna do. We are gonna walk down them stairs, out the front door, and into the street. No funny business."

"You're the boss," responded Gregory.

"Damn right, I am!" the rioter grimaced.

Suddenly, a loud gunshot went off, and both men were splattered in blood. The room filled with a thick cloud of gun smoke. Startled, both men examined themselves and each other because they had blood on them, but they weren't hurt. When the smoke settled, they saw the rioter's body on the floor, with blood pouring from a large hole in the back of his head. Standing above the corpse--was Mr. Mitchell, holding his smoking shotgun.

"Papa," said Gregory, laughing with relief, "Your timing has never been better.

"Don't relax yet," answered Mr. Mitchell. "I smell smoke."

"It's from your gun, right?" asked Willy.

"No, wait a minute," interjected Gregory. "This fool said that left something cooking. He must have set the kitchen on fire!"

"Damn you!" Willy screamed at the corpse, kicking it. "You took everything from us!"

"No time for that, Willy," said Mr. Mitchell. "We need to get out of here now!" As Mr. Mitchell grasped Willy's arm, Willy spat on the corpse as Mr. Mitchell led him from the room.

"Papa," asked Gregory, "How much ammunition do we have left?"

"Plenty for the rifle and my shotgun, but the only pistol bullets we have left are those left in Willy's gun."

"I think I have five," answered Willy.

"How many are still out there?"asked Mr. Mitchell.

"Three that we know about," said Gregory. "I don't know how many more are coming. After all, half the block is burning right now."

"So, when he leave here, we need to be prepared for anything."

"You said it, Papa."

 Once they reached the stairs, the three men looked towards the dining room. It was overwhelmed with black smoke, and the entire kitchen and Lela-Ann's bedroom were burning. The invasive orange flames began to permeate the dining room as the smoke entered the hallway. The smoke began to enter their nasal passages.

"Let's go," said Mr. Mitchell, coughing.

"You still in there, Jimmy?" they heard a voice outside accompanied by steps. "Come on out; the damn place is burning. "

The door swung open, presenting a tall, long-haired man with a drooping mustache. His face dropped and grew pale with fear as he saw three Colored men pointing guns at him. Before he could say or do anything, the three men opened fire. When the man's lifeless body collapsed, Willy reached over to check him for weapons, but Mr. Mitchell stopped him.

"Don't," Mr. Mitchell said. "We don't have time."

He barely finished his sentence when they heard the chandelier crash onto the dining room floor. Mr. Mitchell and Junior spent hours together assembling it the day before the latter began high school. The blue brocade curtains were now melted beads and ash. The wallpaper crumbled from the walls, and from the ceiling fell plaster and burning wood. The beautiful dining room Mrs. Mitchell took so much pride in was reduced to ashes, a pillar of fire, and billowing smoke.

"Willy," Gregory broke the silence, as the men started walking towards the door with extreme caution, "You mind if I drive?"

"Go ahead, man," Willy handed him the key.

"Our Father, which art in Heaven," Mr. Mitchell began praying as he aimed his shotgun outdoors, started to exit. "Say it with me."

"Hallowed be Thy Name," all three men prayed, guns drawn as they exited. "Thy Kingdom come..."

"There they are!" shouted one of the three remaining rioters.

He fired his pistol without discretion, missing all three of the men. Willy shot him square in the stomach, causing him to topple over in pain. The other two men opened fire on the men, and the men returned fire as they walked backwards to the car. Once they reached the car, which miraculously was unaffected by the night's events, they ran and entered the car.

Once Gregory started the engine, he noticed the remaining two men racing towards the vehicle. Instinctively, Gregory put the vehicle in reverse gear, striking both rioters with the vehicle. He then put the car in drive and stomped on the accelerator. They still heard gunshots as they drove off. When Mr. Mitchell looked back, he saw one of the rioters Gregory hit shooting at the car as he was lying on the ground. He also saw his beautiful house completely covered in flames. He saw every house on his block suffering similar fates. He saw dead bodies strewn on the street. They were Colored, and they were White. They were men, and they were children--even babies. In the horizon, he saw Mount Zion Baptist Church on fire. Even as tears streamed down his face as he mourned the loss of his beautiful, prosperous Greenwood, he struggled to keep his composure.

As he looked into the sky, he wondered why there were stars. Why did God allow the stars to twinkle on such a dreadful, bloody night? Greenwood was a community devoted to Him. Should not His tears fall on such a night and wash away the spilt blood and fires of hate? Or is the Curse of Ham truly upon them? Alas, no matter how much he prayed and adhered to the Protestant Ethic, did God truly think of him and all Coloreds the way the lynch mobs did--as a nigger?

As Mr. Mitchell continued to gaze at the sky he saw three airplanes hovering over Greenwood.

"Gregory," he asked, "Is that the National Guard?" Gregory looked up as he drove.

"I doubt it," Gregory answered. "Hold on; those look like the planes they built for the War but never used."

As they looked on, they saw mysterious items being dropped from one of the planes. The second plane also dropped materials, and then the third. The mysterious materials burst into flames when they landed on rooftops.

"I just can't believe it," Gregory said, shaking his head as he sped away. "They wanted the whole neighborhood destroyed. Heathens! We're almost out of Tulsa, and then we'll be safe. And don't worry, Willy! I'm sure my folks will be able to keep you until you get back to your own kin, all right?" He turned back to face Willy, who did not answer him. Willy was winching and groaning in pain. "Willy, what's wrong?" Mr. Mitchell turned to him as well.

"I don't know," Willy struggled to respond.

"Willy," Mr. Mitchell spoke up apprehensively, "You're bleeding!" He pointed to Willy's soaked shirt. He reached over and unbuttoned it, opening it wide. Blood was oozing from Willy's left shoulder. He turned to Gregory, who faced the road again "He's been shot!"

"Put some pressure on the wound," Gregory replied. "It'll stop the bleeding till we get him to a hospital. The closest one from here is a mile down from my folks' house."

"Ah'll be all right," Willy said weakly.

"Don't talk, son," Mr. Mitchell said softly. He removed his blazer and held it securely to his wound. "Just take it easy." He looked up at Gregory. "Someone must have shot him before we got in the car."

    Gregory drove as quickly as he ever drove before to get to safety and to get help for Willy. When they were 20 minutes out of town, he looked around and saw nothing but stars. He could barely even see the fire from Greenwood, and there was a silence he had not heard in what seemed to be a lifetime.

"We made it, y'all!" Gregory called to Willy and Mr. Mitchell in the back.

"You hear that, son?" Mr. Mitchell feigned to smile as he continued holding his jacket over Willy's shoulder. He did not answer or make a noise. "Willy? Did you hear me?" He tapped Willy's good shoulder. Still no answer. "Willy!"

    Mr. Mitchell shook him, causing his head to fall forwards. Mr. Mitchell placed his hand under Willy's chin and lifted his head. Mr. Mitchell's entire body shook with grief. While Willy's body was stiff, his eyes were completely open.

"Is Willy okay?" Gregory asked.

"He is more than okay," Mr. Mitchell sullenly answered, his right hand putting away his jacket and his left hand closing Willy's eyes. "He's gone to the Lord."

Shocked, Gregory put the car on brake and looked back. Upon seeing Willy's lifeless body slumped against the car's interior, he leaned back over the steering wheel, sobbing loudly, striking his temples with his hands.

"Damn, damn, damn!" he cried. "Damn them to hell! I wish I would have shot more of those bastards! I wish I would have burned down THEIR buildings!" Mr. Mitchell reached over and pulled Gregory's hands from his head to keep him from hurting himself. He wrapped his arms around Gregory in a hug.

"Cry if you need to son," Mr. Mitchell comforted him. "Just try to keep it down, lest the wrong people should hear you."

"I don't care anymore," Gregory said between sobs.

"Well, I do. We were fortunate to get out alive. At least you're not injured, and my arm is going to be fine. I don't want to risk that. Our women need us, son." At this, Gregory was able to calm himself.

"You're right. I just wish I had a chance to thank him."

"I'm sure he knew. Besides, I bet he would have wanted to thank you for how you gave him the chance to fight next to a war hero. I'm sure this was the most proud night for him."

"He was quite a soldier himself." said Gregory as he drove away.

Chapter 6:
The Phoenix Will Rise

As the sun rose over Owasso, all was quiet and peaceful. The rooster from a nearby farm crowed as he would on a regular day, and so did the many birds. The gentle breeze and the absence of clouds promised another beautiful day, and all of nature seemed to rejoice at such a prospect.

At the Willborn home, however, everyone was unaffected by the glory of spring. Mrs. Mitchell, Phyllis, and Lela-Ann sat silently on the porch looking out onto the road's horizon. They had made it safely and without incident out of Tulsa, but they had heard stories already about the fires and killings of Greenwood, and they waited restlessly to learn if their men had made it out alive. Lela-Ann was very despondent and bereft of emotion, while Mrs. Mitchell devoted her vigil to deep prayer. Between them was Phyllis, eyes puffy and red, face stained with the many un-wiped tears long dried. She was fearful that she lost her father and fiancé on the same night and was uncertain of her future. Even with Lela-Ann and her mother wrapping their arms around her, she could not feel comfort.

"I see y'all couldn't sleep either," said Mrs. Willborn as she stepped out onto the porch. "We couldn't either. James is making us some coffee."

"I thought they would be here by now," said Mrs. Mitchell wryly, staring into space. "I told that foolish man to forget the house, but he wouldn't listen. Him and his stubborn pride! What good is a house without a husband?"

"Papa! Gregory!" Phyllis weakly sobbed.

"Phyllis, please try to get ahold of yourself!" Mrs. Mitchell scolded, still looking down the road. Realizing her words, she faced her daughter with pity. "I'm sorry. I didn't mean that. I'm frightened too. Have you prayed?"

"Yes, ma'am."

"Then keep praying and put your trust in Jesus. That's the best and only thing."

"It sho' is in God's hands now," Lela-Ann said, almost in a whisper."

"We thank you for your hospitality," Mrs. Mitchell looked up at Mrs. Willborn. "I only regret that we were not introduced in more pleasant circumstances."

"It's all right," Mrs. Willborn assured the women. "But don't call me Mrs. Willborn. We're kin now. Call me Marjorie."

"Thank you, Marjorie. My name is Violet."

"And, Phyllis," Mrs. Willborn turned to her, "I was hoping to meet you soon. Gregory was so excited when he called and told me y'all were engaged." Her voice began to crack as tears started to flow. "Lord, I hope that boy's safe." An older man, bald, joined the women on the porch, carrying a tray of coffee, a 10-year-old girl, Gregory's sister, walking behind him with cups. He placed the coffee on the wicker table and wrapped his arms around Mrs. Willborn.

"Come on, darlin'," he comforted her. "That boy is too smart and too clever. He's a Corporal. Millions of Germans couldn't stop him. He'll be fine."

"Lord willing," said Lela-Ann.

    As if prophecy, everyone saw the black dot of a car far down the road. And then it came closer. And closer. In anticipation, Phyllis leaped out of her seat and ran to the road. The car kept coming closer, but it was hard to tell who the passengers were.

As she waited in anxious hope, Mrs. Mitchell and Lela-Ann, both curious, joined her by the road, with the Willborn's close behind. Phyllis intently scanned the car in the road, studying the faces inside of it. She knew it was probably a random driver, but she reasoned with herself that it was still too early for people to travel. As Phyllis continued examining the faces in the car, she prayed hard as her mother advised her. When the car was halfway up the block, her face brightened to recognize two similar faces.

"It's them!" she rejoiced. "It's them!"

Mrs. Mitchell looked harder and then clasped her hands in intense relief.

"It is them!" she exclaimed. "Clarence!"

"God be praised," said Lela-Ann with an exhausted smile.

"Gregory!" Mrs. Willborn shouted, wrapping her arm around her husband.

"I told you he'd make it, woman!" Mr. Willborn responded as tears streamed down his eyes. "I told you!"

When the car finally approached the happy crowd, it stopped in front of them with a screech. Mr. Mitchell and Gregory hurried out of the car and ran to their family. Mrs. Mitchell ran to her husband, and they held on tight to each other, as if they would never let go, crying together. Phyllis and Gregory squeezed onto each other as if they were away from each other for years. Gregory then picked up his Phyllis and they kissed each other with all the passion within them.

Gregory noticed his sobbing mother and put Phyllis down, who then ran and embraced her father.

"It's fine, Mama," said Gregory, holding his mother. "I'm fine." Mr. Willborn and his daughter came over and joined the hug.

"Praise Jesus," cried Lela-Ann, wrapping her arms around Mr. Mitchell, who hugged her back. They then walked back to the porch together.

"Y'all must be hungry," declared Mrs. Willborn, wiping her eyes. "I'll make breakfast." She turned to the girl, "Cleotha, come help me."

"Yes, ma'am," Cleotha answered, following her mother into the house.

"Sit on down, " invited Mr. Willborn, handing Mr. Mitchell a cigar."

"Thank you, sir," Mr. Mitchell accepted the cigar, and Mr. Willborn lit it for him. Mr. Willborn then lit a cigar for himself.

"Name's James."

"James."

"So, what happened with y'all?" Mr. Willborn asked Gregory, handing him a cigar and lighting it for him. "It's about that Rowland boy. That I know."

"Papa," answered Gregory, "a mob of armed White men who were bent on hanging Rowland stood at the courthouse, and they wouldn't go away like the Sherriff told them. An attachment of veterans went to help him, but he told us to go home. We started to leave, but they hassled us and tried to take one man's gun. There was a shot, and we just started shooting at one another. We escaped to Greenwood, but they followed us and started burning buildings. They killed every Colored they found, even if they surrendered. If we hadn't stopped them, they would have dragged an old man, a neighbor to death, and they would have cut a baby out of a woman's stomach. It was damn awful. "

"Um-um-um," Mr. Willborn shook his head.

"I regret to inform you, my dear," Mr. Mitchell looked at his wife, "that we couldn't save the house. It burned down. We've lost everything."

"Forget about all that," she gently told her husband, stroking his head. "We still have each other, we are safe, and that's all that matters." She looked around. "But where is Willy, though? I thought he stayed with you. Did he go back with his family?"

"Violet, Willy is...he's..." He became tongue tied.

"Willy is dead," Gregory spoke up. "He was so brave and dedicated to helping us that he didn't even realize he had been shot in the shoulder, a cut above his heart. Must have hit an artery because we couldn't stop the bleeding. We buried him a few miles out of town and piled some stones over so that we could find it when, or if, anyone in his family should ask after him."

    Everyone kept silence for a few minutes to reflect on Willy and all that transpired in the hours that passed.

"Well," Mr. Willborn broke the silence, "I don't know what y'all plan to do, but you can stay here as long as you need to get back on your feet."

"Thank you, James," answered Mr. Mitchell. "I certainly promise you that we won't be a burden to you for long. We will be leaving here soon enough."

"What do you mean, Clarence?" Mrs. Mitchell asked.

"We are going back."

"Back where?"

"Back home. Back to Greenwood."

"Greenwood? Clarence, you're not thinking straight. You are tired and hungry. You can't mean that."

"I do mean it. We are going back."

"Clarence, be realistic! There is no Greenwood. Not anymore. Go back to what? Rubble and monsters who hate us?"

"You are wrong," Mr. Mitchell raised his voice, standing up. "There will always be Greenwood! The hopes and dreams are in Greenwood. The spirit of our people is there! So is everything my daddy taught me, and everything my granddaddy was whipped for as a slave and died for. There will always be Greenwood. They can hate us all they want, but we will take what's ours! It might be rubble, but it's ours. It's ours! And we will claim it! They may have destroyed it, but we will resurrect it again and make it better. We will show them what we can do. They may destroy what we create, but they cannot destroy us! And, Violet, we will rebuild. As God as my witness, we will rebuild!

Epilogue

The Tulsa Race Riot of 1921 claimed the lives of approximately 400 people--300 African American, and 100 White. Even the famous surgeon, Dr. A.C. Jackson, was shot and killed in front of his house as he surrendered to a mob. O.W. Turley, rumored to have been lynched by a mob, escaped to California and never returned to Greenwood, dying a few years later. Hundreds of others were injured, and thousands were arrested and placed into detention camps around the city, possibly for their protection. The Red Cross came to Tulsa and built tents for them to stay in until the state of emergency ended.

The Greenwood residents defended themselves well against rioters and looters, but their efforts became futile as homes and buildings burned, especially by airplanes flying over the neighborhood, dropping incendiary bombs and turpentine on buildings. While it is unknown who flew the planes, some have suspected Tulsa police while others believe it was the National Guard. In either case, nearly every home, business, and church were destroyed. The estimated damages to real estate cost $1.5 million and $750,000 in private property, both figures in 1921 dollars. Of all those who filed insurance claims for their losses, essentially none of them received compensation.

The charges against Dick Rowland were dropped, and he left Tulsa immediately after being freed, relocating to Kansas City. Little is known about his life thereafter.

While some Greenwood residents never returned to their community, most of them did. Faced by opposition by some prominent members of Tulsa who were members of the local Ku Klux Klan, including Wyatt Tate Brady, Greenwood survivors sued Tulsa and was allowed to rebuild their community, making it even more prosperous than it was before the riot.

This Jim Crow-segregated neighborhood continued to flourish until the height of the Civil Rights Movement, in which African-American residents finally were able to patronize stores and businesses outside of their communities. Still, every African American with a dream and the courage to work hard to bring it to fruition carries Greenwood in their hearts. History has proven we are capable of raising ourselves from fieldwork to finance and from mammies to millionaires. If we work together, we can be and do anything.

Dedicated to the memory of the approximately 300 residents of Greenwood:

Ed Adams	*Edward G. Howard*	*M.M. Sandridge*
Greg Alexander	*Billy Hudson*	*Lewis Shelton*
Harry Barker	*Dr. Andrew C. Jackson*	*Nelson Talbot*
Howard Barrens	*George Jeffery*	*Eliza Talbot*
Tom Bryant	*Ed Lockard*	*William Turner*
Carrie Diamond	*Joe Miller*	*Cualey Walker*
Ruben Everett	*S.H. Pierce*	*Henry Walker*
George Hawkins	*Sam Ree*	*John Wheeler*

Plus hundreds of other men, women, and children who could not be identified

as well as to the survivors who did not surrender to despair but rebuilt their homes and started over. May your efforts never be left in vain.

Acknowledgements

A special thank you to the congregants of Vernon African Methodist Episcopal Church for sending me the picture of their church, one of the few buildings to survive the riot.

To the Greenwood Cultural Center for giving me a lead to a resource needed to complete this book.

To the Oklahoma Historical Society for patiently answering my questions and providing resources.

To Alex Bohanan for giving me permission to use her picture.

To Harriet Bohanan for expressing her interest in the book.

To the trailblazers on both sides of my family who lived with dignity and hope.

To the memories of the first residents of Ivan, Arkansas, who built a hamlet on my family's land.

To the many Euro-American philanthropists and benefactors who built colleges for us when we were not allowed in established academies and who hid us and helped us escape in times of trouble.

(Dr. A.C. Jackson, shot dead after surrendering to mob)

(Vernon AME Church, one of the only surviving structures.)
(Alex Bohanan, 2018. Used with permission)

(Vernon AME Church, 2018. Used with permission)

All photographs in black and white were taken before 1923 and are therefore under Public Domain.

Lightning Source UK Ltd.
Milton Keynes UK
UKHW011237161020
371707UK00001B/63